Table of Contents

Ghosts of the Empyrium

Cover design by Alysabeth Vale
Interior design by Alysabeth Vale
ISBN: 979-8-9945284-1-9

The Empyrium Chronicles: ARC 1
Book 1:
Ghosts of the Empyrium

The tyrant's son. The rebel's daughter.
Two ghosts, one fire to burn the world clean

Dedication:

For Aly—and the girl who built her.
Both of us made it out

RITUAL GATE: THE GATE OF FIRST WOUNDS

✦ ☽⋆☾ ✦

Before you enter, know this:
The world you're about to step into carries sharp edges.
People are broken here.
People hurt.
People survive things they shouldn't have had to.
If you continue, walk gently.
Some wounds look like fiction,
but they came from somewhere real.

Part I

Origins & Echoes

"Before destiny binds, it whispers."

Chapter 1: Lessons of Steel

Tiberius · Age 16

The training hall smells like metal and ozone—

the scent of my childhood.

My father stands behind me, his steps echoing like a countdown.

Most people call him *Dominion*, ruler of the Empire.

I call him *sir*.

I'm not sure he's ever called me *son*.

"Again," he orders.

The word hits harder than the shock-rod will.

I tighten my grip on the practice blade. My palms are already sore, skin rubbed raw from drills before dawn. The Ion Veil glows through the narrow windows, its electric blue bleeding across the steel floor. The color makes my scars look fresh.

I strike the drone.

Too slow. I already know it.

"Your left wrist hesitated."

My stomach drops. "It didn't, Fa—sir."

The correction comes too late.

The shock-rod cracks across my shoulder and white-hot electricity tears through me. My knees buckle; the floor meets me hard. A small sound escapes—barely—but it does.

Father hears it.

He always hears everything.

His voice is calm. Controlled.

Unlike me.

"Hesitation is death, Tiberius."

My muscles twitch uncontrollably from the jolt. "I won't hesitate again."

"You will," he says. "Because you still think like a child."

Something bruises in my chest. I keep my face blank.

He circles me, hands clasped behind his back, calm in that clinical way that always means danger.

"Children expect mercy, fairness, meaning. Do you?"

I swallow. "No, sir."

He stops behind me. I feel the cold of him before he speaks.

"In this world, love is earned through usefulness."

My fingers tighten on the blade. The metal digs into my skin. "Yes, sir."

"Rise."

I push myself up too fast, shoulder screaming from the shock, vision pulsing black at the edges. I hope he doesn't notice the wobble in my knees.

He notices everything.

The drone resets with a metallic click.

"Begin."

I strike again. Harder. Faster. My breaths come shorter. My hands tremble even as I force them still. I hit every mark, but he doesn't nod. He doesn't blink.

He never shows approval.

Not really.

And god help me—

I still want it.

I push past the burn. Past the shaking. Past the lingering sting of electricity. I push because if I give less than perfect, I disappear.

Finally, Father steps forward and catches the drone's arm mid-cycle. He doesn't flinch as the metal grinds inches from his wrist.

"What do you feel?" he asks softly.

His soft voice is worse than shouting.

My throat tightens.

Fear. Pain. Desperation.

Hope that he'll say *good* just once.

I smother all of it.

"Purpose."

A flicker passes through his eyes. Not warmth—just calculation.

"Good," he says.

He touches the side of my face—not gently, not harshly, just claiming what he owns.

"My son must be strong. Stronger than weakness. Stronger than himself."

My heart stutters at the word *son*.

He rarely uses it.

He always uses it when he wants something more from me.

"Yes, Father."

He releases me.

"Again."

I strike until my arms shake uncontrollably. Until sweat blinds me. Until the blade slips from my fingers and I flinch—actually flinch—waiting for the shock-rod.

It doesn't come.

He only watches.

"You are improving," he says at last. "Do not disappoint me tomorrow."

Tomorrow:

Live drills.

Real targets.

Real fear I'm not allowed to feel.

"Yes, Father."

He leaves without another word. The hall seems colder the moment he's gone.

Only then do I let out the breath I've been holding. I press a hand to my shoulder; it throbs under my fingers. My legs feel weak, too weak, but I force them steady anyway.

I bend to pick up the blade. My hands won't stop shaking.

I'm not a weapon yet.

But he's determined to make me one.

And I'm terrified of what will happen when I finally stop being afraid.

Hesitation kills.

Obedience keeps me alive.

Control keeps him proud.

Perfection earns love.

These are the lessons of steel.

The only inheritance I'll ever get.

I straighten my spine, swallow the ache, and walk out of the hall.

Tomorrow, I cannot fail.

Usefulness earns love.

Hesitation earns pain.

I don't know what happens to sons who fail him—

and I don't want to find out.

✦ ☽⋆☾ ✦

Rain sharpens everything.

Every sound. Every breath.

Every mistake I cannot allow myself to make.

It beads on my gloves as I stand above the ruined warehouse, watching my drones hover in formation below. Dominion's voice echoes in my skull—not through comms, but memory.

Hesitation kills, Tiberius.

Precision saves.

My heartbeat stays steady. It always does.

"Commander Braxton," Lieutenant Hale says beside me, visor reflecting streaks of neon through the storm. "Rebel sweep team confirmed. Authorization?"

"Containment."

My voice lands like a blade.

He repeats it into the line. The drones descend.

Below, movement flares—shadows scrambling through the broken skeleton of the warehouse. Young. Too young. They all are. The rebels send children because they run faster and die quieter.

Drones fire. Targets fall.

Efficient. Clean.

But one of them doesn't fall.

A girl—small, fast, face half-hidden under a hood—shoves another kid behind cover, taking the hit on her shoulder and firing back with a snarl that cuts through the storm. She moves like she's been surviving her whole life.

My throat tightens—

Don't hesitate, Tiberius.

I don't.

"Focus fire," I command.

The drones adjust instantly.

The girl lifts her gaze toward me.

And everything slows.

Her eyes lock with mine across the distance—

dark, burning, furious.

Not fear.

Recognition. Her hood is soaked, her eyes wild, but I doubt she can see mine through the downpour.

Something in my chest drops hard.

She looks at me like I'm the monster under her bed.

Maybe I am.

She pulls another rebel—another child—behind her. Protecting them. Even knowing she's already lost.

A flash of plasma hits the girl beside her.

The scream rips through the hall.

The protector hits her knees, catching the dying body like she knows it's her fault for not being stronger. Rain splatters in the blood pooling between her hands.

Something inside me splinters.

"Commander?" Hale prompts. "Orders?"

A command waits on my tongue—Stop. Cease fire. Let her go.

I don't say it. I don't break the rule.

"Finish it."

The words taste like iron.

The last of the rebels fall. Except her.

She stands, shaking, drenched in rain and blood, and raises her weapon at me with a scream that shouldn't come from a child. She kills two drones cleanly.

A third with her bare hands. Her first kills.

She doesn't look away from me once.

My pulse stutters.

I never stutter.

"Commander," Hale says quietly. "She's still alive."

I should order her execution.

But instead, without thinking—"Withdraw."

Hale stiffens. "Sir?"

"I said withdraw."

The drones rise. My officers regroup. Boots slap through puddles as we step out into the open street. I don't look back.

I *can't* look back.

If I do, I'll see her kneeling in the wreckage again.

And I'll feel that hesitation again.

The one Dominion trained out of me years ago.
Control equals safety.
Obedience equals love.
So why did I disobey?
Why did I let *her* live?
The storm lashes harder. The Ion Veil hums overhead like a warning.
Hesitation kills.
But today, hesitating spared a girl who refused to fall.
As I walk into the rain, one truth curls cold and sharp inside me:
I will see that girl again.
And when I do...
I don't know which of us will destroy the other.

Chapter 2: Blood in the Rain

Aly · Age 16

The rain tastes like metal.

It coats my teeth, my tongue, my throat as we move through the ruins like ghosts pretending to be soldiers. Beneath the Ion Veil, the sky bleeds neon, staining the puddles at our feet an unnatural blue.

"Routine sweep," Command said.

Routine.

Nothing about this war is routine.

Mara walks just behind me, her breath steady but her fingers twitching around her rifle. She's been like a sister since we were twelve—joking, stubborn, fearless. Tonight she feels breakable.

Or maybe that's just me.

"Kye, cover the west," I whisper. "We'll sweep the interior."

He nods once, jaw tight.

We step into the broken warehouse. Half a roof. Collapsed beams. The husk of machines scattered like bones. I flick my wrist-light on. Dust swirls in the beam.

"Grab the drives fast. In and out. Ten—"

The floor hums.

My heart stops.

"Mara—"

The ceiling explodes.

A scream tears the air open as metal shrapnel rains down. The blast hurls me sideways. My shoulder slams into concrete. The shock knocks the air out of me.

Drones flood through the hole like a swarm of metal locusts, wings whirring, lights snapping red.

"No—NO—"

My hands scramble for my rifle.

"DOWN!" I shout, throat raw.

Mara dives behind a support beam with me. Kye isn't fast enough. A plasma bolt hits him square in the chest. His body jerks—

and he collapses.

"KYE!"

My voice cracks.

Another blast hits the wall near his head. He doesn't move again.

The drones descend relentlessly.

Mara fires until her arms shake. I fire with her. Each shot lights up the dark. The recoil shudders through my bones. The air stinks of ozone and burning metal.

"Reload!" Mara shouts.

"I'm trying—"

A drone screams past my ear. The heat sears my cheek. I roll, slam my back into concrete, and shoot it point-blank. Sparks shower the floor.

Another drone drops from above—and then the world... shifts.

I sense him before I see him.

A shape framed in the ripped-out wall, rain pouring behind him like a curtain of blue fire. A boy-shaped silhouette standing on a fallen beam like it's a stage built for nightmares.

Black coat. Dark gloves.

Calm in the chaos.

I can't see his face—only the cruel stillness of someone untouched by the storm he commands.

A chill runs through me.

The Ghost of the Empire.

Not fact—just fear.

A rumor with a pulse.

A shadow with a kill-count.

Our gazes collide—or maybe I just feel him looking at me.

Hard to tell through the rain and smoke.

He lifts a hand.

All the drones stop mid-air.

A breath of silence.

One heartbeat.

Two—

"Finish it."

His voice is emotionless.

Mechanical.

Like death learned how to speak.

The next blast rips through Mara.

She jerks violently, her body crashing into mine. Her rifle slips from her hands. She gasps—a wet, broken sound I feel all the way to my spine.

"Mara—Mara—NO—"

I drop to my knees with her, hands scrambling, useless.

Warm blood pours between my fingers.

Her eyes find mine.

Wide. Shining. Scared.

She tries to speak—but only blood comes out.

"Please," I whisper.

"I'm right here. I'm right—Mara—don't—"

Her chest rises once.

Falls. Still.

Something shatters inside me.

My breath stutters violently. My vision blurs from rain and tears and the sting of smoke. The world narrows to the sound of drones whirring overhead like vultures.

My fingers slip from her cooling skin.

Then something inside me ignites.

I grab her rifle with shaking hands, rise on legs that barely hold, and fire at the nearest drone with a scream that tears my throat raw.

One drops.

Then another.

Then another.

I shoot until the gun clicks empty.

Until my arms burn.

Until my grief becomes fury and my fury becomes survival.

A drone lunges at me.

Too fast. Too close.

I swing the butt of the rifle into its core with all the strength I have left. It cracks open, sparks spewing like dying stars.

My first kill.

It feels like the world breaking.

When the last drone hits the ground, the warehouse falls silent except for the hiss of rain through the broken roof.

He's still there.

The silhouette on the beam.

Unmoved.

Untouched.

Unbothered.

He steps down slowly, calmly, like none of this is worth rushing for. Water drips from his gloves. His coat is pristine except for the rain.

He doesn't look like a boy.

He looks like a verdict.

His shadowed gaze finds me.

I freeze—just for a breath.

Just long enough to feel the weight of being... seen.

Marked. Remembered. He turns away.

"Withdraw," he orders. "We're done."

Done.

He walks out as if the dead around me are nothing more than clutter he's stepping around.

My legs give out.

I collapse beside Mara—what's left of her—pressing my forehead to her shoulder, shaking as rain washes the blood across the floor in thin, red rivers.

"I'm sorry," I whisper.

"I'm so—so sorry."

My heart feels like shrapnel lodged in my ribs.

I lift my head and watch the silhouette vanish into the storm he made.

Something sharp settles in my chest—heavy, cold, unyielding.

A promise forged in blood and rain.

I won't forget this.

I won't forgive him.

Not now.

Not ever.

Chapter 3: The Tavern Whispers

Aly

I shouldn't be here.

I should be reporting back to Command, telling them that my squad—my friends—are gone.

That Mara died in my arms.

That Kye didn't even get a final word.

But halfway there, something inside me cracked.

My feet stopped.

My breath went thin.

And suddenly I was standing in the market rings, surrounded by noise and strangers and life I couldn't bear to face.

So I stepped into the first place loud enough to drown the screaming in my head.

A tavern.

Mother would hate it.

But if she knew what happened tonight...

I think she'd forgive me for needing a place that wasn't silent.

My hands won't stop shaking as I sink into a booth in the shadowed corner. My shoulder burns from the drone hit, my ribs throb with every breath. The tavern keeper drops a mug of broth in front of me, muttering something about "haunted eyes."

He doesn't know how right he is.

I sip it just to feel something warm.

Something alive.

Then a nearby table erupts with laughter—Empyrium soldiers, off-duty, half-drunk, smug.

My body goes rigid.

I angle myself deeper into the shadows, hood low.

The men keep talking.

"...should be here any second," one says, glancing toward the door. "He always checks the rings before heading back to the central sectors."

"Dominion likes his little prince seen," another snorts. "Keeps everyone scared."

Prince.

My pulse stutters.

"We get the scraps," a younger soldier grumbles. "He gets the glory."

"Glory?" the older man laughs. "Call it what it is: killing. Street cleaning. Ghost work."

Ghost work?

I lean a fraction closer without meaning to.

"You didn't see him in Sector Twelve," the first soldier says, voice dropping. "The ruler's son himself—cleaned the streets of rebels in under five minutes. Didn't even flinch."

Ice floods my veins.

Ruler's son.

Sector Twelve.

Didn't flinch.

Are they... talking about—

"Oh yeah," the younger man says. "The stories don't do him justice. The Ghost of the Empire—"

The door slams open.

A gust of cold air sweeps through the tavern, carrying rain and silence with it.

The soldiers snap to attention.

I look up.

And my heart stops.

He steps inside like the storm followed him.

Black coat dampened by rain.

Dark gloves dripping water onto the floor.

Face pale, calm, emotionless.

The silhouette from the warehouse.

But now he has a face—a real one.

A boy's face.

Sixteen. My age.

A boy who shouldn't look this tired.

This empty.

One of the soldiers grins shakily.

"And the Ghost appears."

Ghost.

And the ruler's son.

One and the same.

The truth slams into me so hard my breath catches.

The Ghost of the Empire...

is Dominion's son.

The boy who killed my squad. The boy who said *finish it.*

The boy who hesitated for half a heartbeat.

The boy who walks into a tavern like he's dragging a battlefield behind him.

He moves through the room with quiet precision, nodding once as the soldiers stiffen.

I shrink back into the corner, heart hammering, praying he won't look my way.

He doesn't.

He looks exhausted.

Like the weight of the Empire is on his spine.

Like he hasn't slept in months.

This should make me hate him more.

But instead—

Instead, it makes something inside me twist painfully.

He killed my friends.

He ruined my life in one night.

But now that I see him up close...

He doesn't look like a monster.

He looks like a boy someone carved into a weapon.

A boy who's breaking under the sharp edges.

My breath catches in my throat.

Heat stings my eyes.

I turn away, gripping the edge of the table until my knuckles go white.

I should run.

I should hate him.

I should want him dead.

But for one horrifying moment...

I just feel sorry for him.

And that scares me more than anything.

I slip out of the booth, keeping my hood low, heart pounding like it's trying to escape my chest.

I can't be here.

Not with him.

Not like this.

I push through the tavern door into the cold, rain-slicked night—

and every step away from him feels like a step toward something I don't understand yet.

Something I'm not sure I'm ready for.

But one thing is certain: I'll never forget his face.

And now that I know who he is—I'm not sure I'll ever forgive him.

Not now.

Not ever.

Chapter 4: Ash and Echo

Aly

The Undergrid smells like damp metal and burnt circuits—like a graveyard for machines and people alike.

I move through the tunnels in a daze, the fluorescent strips flickering overhead. Every step echoes too loud. Every breath hurts. The air feels too thin for lungs still full of smoke and screaming.

Beneath the rebellion's teeth and grit, the Undergrid has always been home.

Tonight it feels like a coffin.

Two guards spot me, their eyes widening as they take in the blood, the bruising, the way I can't quite meet their gaze.

"Aly—Commander Carmichael wants you in the war room. Now."

Of course she does.

I square my shoulders, swallowing the burn in my throat.

Mother doesn't tolerate weakness.

Tonight she'll see nothing but.

The door slides open.

Faces turn toward me.

Generals. Medics. Strategists.

My mother at the head of the table, steel-backed and sharp-eyed in her dark coat.

Relief flickers in her expression—gone in an instant.

"Alysa." Her voice is stern. Controlled.

"Report."

My legs tremble as I step forward, but I force them steady.

"Our sweep team was ambushed," I say. "Drones. Heavy fire. They were waiting for us."

A ripple of tension moves through the room.

Mother's jaw tightens. "And your squad?"

My throat closes.

I stare at the floor.

"Gone."

Silence.

Heavy. Suffocating.

One of the generals slams his palm onto the table. "You should have fallen back. Why didn't you signal for reinforcements?"

My hands curl into fists. "There was no time."

"You expect us to believe that?" another snaps. "A good soldier prioritizes the mission—"

"They were my friends," I fire back before I can stop myself. "I wasn't going to leave them."

The room erupts into layered voices—accusations, disappointment, strategy notes spoken like eulogies.

Finally Mother raises her hand.

Silence falls instantly.

Her eyes lock onto mine—cool, assessing, sharp enough to pierce bone.

"Aly," she says softly. Too softly. "Compassion has a place. But not on the battlefield."

"That wasn't compassion," I whisper. "It was survival."

"You hesitated," a general says.

Like it's a sin. Like hesitation should mean death.

I feel the words like a slap.

Mother studies me carefully. "Your mercy is becoming a weakness."

Heat rises up my neck.

If only they knew what I could have done in the tavern.

If only they knew who I saw there.

Who walked through those doors, soaked in rain and exhaustion.

I could have ended him.

I could have shot him point-blank and avenged Mara.

But I didn't.

And I don't know why.

Maybe I do.

Maybe that's what terrifies me.

Mother sighs—barely audible. "We will discuss new placement for you tomorrow. Everyone is dismissed."

Her tone says *failure.*

Her eyes say *prove you're worth saving.*

I bow my head.

"We'll regroup. We'll recover stronger."

It's the answer she wants.

Obedience with sharp edges.

Inside, all I want is to scream.

I turn to leave, but hear quick footsteps behind me then I feel my mother's hand closes around my arm.

"Stay."

The room empties, doors sliding shut behind the last general.

Her composure cracks—just barely.

"Aly..."

Her voice breaks on my name.

She steps closer, brushing dust from my cheek like I'm still a child who scraped her knees.

"I'm sorry," she says softly. "I know what they meant to you."

My throat tightens painfully.

"I should've tried harder," I whisper. "I should've—"

"No." She grips my chin gently, making me meet her eyes.

"This war kills children. You survived. Do you understand what a miracle that is?"

Tears sting my eyes.

But crying now feels like betrayal.

Mother smooth's my hair back, her touch gentle in a way I rarely see.

"You are strong, Aly. But your heart... it will get you hurt."

I want to tell her everything—about the Ghost, about the tavern, about how he didn't look like a monster at all, about how that fact is ruining me.

But I don't.

I swallow the truth like a stone.

Her hands drop from my face. "Go rest."

I nod stiffly, throat burning.

"Wait," she says.

I stop.

For a moment, she just looks at me—not like a commander weighing assets, but like a woman counting what she has left. Then she reaches into the inside pocket of her coat and presses something into my palm.

It's cool. Solid.

A compass.

Old. Scratched. The casing worn smooth in places like it's been handled more than it's been admired.

"I carried this longer than you've been alive," she says quietly. "Long enough to forget I ever needed it."

I frown down at it. "Why give it to me?"

"Because you don't confuse direction with obedience," she replies. "And because when this war gets louder—and it will—you'll need something that doesn't."

I turn it over. My breath catches.

My name is etched into the back.

*Aly—

To remind you were true north is when everyone around you is lying.*

I look up, startled.

She closes my fingers around it before I can speak. Her hand lingers there, firm and steady.

"I don't trust the council," she says. "I don't trust half the people in that room."

Her eyes meet mine, sharp and unflinching.

"But I trust you."

The words land heavier than any title.

"You see what others won't," she continues. "You hesitate when it matters. You choose people over optics."

She lifts her chin slightly. "That makes you dangerous. And it makes you mine."

My chest tightens.

"Not as a soldier," she adds. "As my right hand."

The room feels smaller suddenly. Quieter.

"I don't need you to be ruthless," she says. "I need you to remember who we are when this tries to turn us into something else."

She releases my hand.

"Keep it," she says. "And keep your silence when it tells you to. You've always known when not to speak."

I close my fingers around the compass, the metal biting just enough to be real.

"I won't lose it," I say.

She gives a small, tired smile. "I know. Now go rest."

I nod, eyes blurring.

Outside the room, a tall figure waits by the dim lights of the corridor.

Kai Virel.

He's leaning against the wall with a datapad under one arm, dark hair half-shadowing his eyes. Older than me by a few years, quiet enough you forget he's a strategist until he speaks.

He straightens when he sees my face.

"A rough night," he says gently.

I blink at him, surprised he isn't barking orders or delivering judgment.

"You heard?" I rasp.

"Everyone heard."

He hesitates, then holds out a clean cloth.

"For the blood."

I take it with shaking fingers.

He studies me—not with pity, not with disappointment, but with something softer.

Something like understanding.

"The bravest soldiers aren't the ruthless ones," he says. "They're the ones who feel everything and still stand."

I swallow hard. "The generals don't agree."

He huffs a quiet breath. "They confuse cruelty with strength."

His gaze flickers over my bruised knuckles, my trembling hand.

"You're still standing," he says. "That's what matters."

I nod, throat tight.

He doesn't ask what happened in the tavern.

He doesn't pry.

He just gives a small, solemn bow of his head.

"If you ever need to talk," he murmurs, "I'm here."

Then he slips into the shadows, leaving me with a warmth I haven't felt in hours.

I head down the corridor toward my bunk, Mara's face flashing behind my eyes, Kye's scream echoing, the Ghost's silhouette burned into my memory.

Anger rises again in my chest—hot, hollow, consuming.

Mercy is weakness, they said.
Mercy is what keeps you broken.
No.
Mercy is what makes me *me*.
But I'll never be that powerless again.
Never.
Not on the battlefield.
Not in the tavern. Not anywhere.

I wipe the blood from my cheek, inhale a trembling breath, and whisper into the quiet:

"I'll become stronger. Whatever it takes."

The lights flicker above me, humming like a warning.

But my resolve only hardens.

I walk on, heart burning with grief and something sharper:

A promise forged from ash—
and echo.

Chapter 5: Shadows in Transit

Aly • Age 17

The Ion Veil claws blue lightning across the freighter's hull, each flicker making the metal shiver like it's about to shake apart.

I wedge myself between crates of stolen medkits, forcing my breath steady. The smugglers call the engine hum a lullaby.

Tonight, it sounds like a countdown.

"Three minutes to patrol sector," Jalen calls, a tight edge in his voice. "If the Empire's cranky, we're dead before we blink."

"Cheerful," I mutter, crawling forward. "Let me see the board."

He doesn't bother pretending I shouldn't.

The navigation screen is a mess of red arcs—Empyrium nets tightening like a noose.

I've seen nooses before.

This one's familiar.

"Nullborn camp's just beyond the ridge," Jalen mutters. "If the meds don't get there tonight, half their kids won't make morning."

My jaw locks.

Nullborn.

Children the Empire pretends aren't real.

Children like I would've been—

like I still am,

on paper.

Unregistered. Uncounted.

A ghost by design.

Mother hid me so the Empire couldn't claim me; it turned me into the exact thing they hunt.

"Freighter Emberwing," a clipped voice snaps over comms. "Identify or prepare for detention."

Jalen swears violently. "No, no, no—"

The ship lurches as the patrol net clamps around us.

Lights flash red.

Boards scream warnings.

My pulse spikes so hard I taste blood.

"Move," I hiss, shoving into the co-pilot seat. "Send me the registry port."

He doesn't argue. There's no time.

A holo ad auto-fires overhead, glitching through static before locking onto Empyrium training footage. White-coated soldiers move in practiced unison.

Then—a silhouette slices across the screen.

Sharp. Precise.

A rhythm I feel like a bruise.

Screams.

Mara collapsing in my arms.

A boy on a beam like he owned death.

I shove the memory down, hard.

"Freighter Emberwing," the patrol barks. "Final warning—respond."

"Working on it!" I snap at the air, fingers flying over the cracked holopad.

The stolen Empyrium codes glitch, error out, recompile.

Every second stretches razor-thin.

Jalen grips the controls like they're prayer beads.

"We're dead, Aly. We're—"

"Not yet." My voice shakes, but my hands don't.

"I don't die in nets."

Another error spike.

Another warning chirp.

C'mon.

C'mon.

Just hold—

"Aly—" Jalen's voice cracks.

I slam one final sequence, override the checksum, and—

"Transmit."

The false ID pings through the patrol grid.

I hold my breath until my lungs burn.

Silence. Static.

A heartbeat that feels like ten.

"...Registry confirmed," the patrol officer says flatly. "Continue."

The net releases in a ripple of dying light.

Jalen collapses backward. "Kid, you're—fuck, you're terrifying."

I let out a tremor of a laugh. "Good."

He wipes his face. "Empire's Ghost must be off-duty. If he'd been running that sweep, we'd be vapor."

The name hits harder than the turbulence ever could.

The Empire's Ghost.

My eyes lift to the holo screen, still flickering with soldiers.

That silhouette—blurred, glitching, but unmistakable.

My skin prickles with cold.

Not again.

Not him.

"Never seen the guy," Jalen rambles, oblivious. "But rumor says he's faster than drones and colder than the Veil."

Cold.

Precise.

Rain in human shape.

"Rumor says a lot of things," I say, voice too thin.

He snorts. "Ghosts. Empire loves its myths."

But the hair stands on the back of my neck.

Some myths have teeth.

And I've already been bitten.

The freighter breaks free of the patrol's shadow, streaking toward the Nullborn encampment—scattered lights trembling in the storm.

I pull my hood up.

These kids... they're like me.

Born outside the Empire's gaze.

Surviving anyway.

Being unseen used to make me feel trapped.

Tonight it feels like a weapon.

But as the ship starts its descent, my gaze drifts again to the silhouette on the holo:

The rhythm of that silhouette—steady, deadly, familiar—I know it.

I survived it.

And something tells me I'm going to face it again.

Chapter 6: The Ghost Prince

Tiberius • Age 17

The Observation Tower is too high up for sound.

Down below, the training yards are full—boots striking in perfect rhythm, guns cycling, voices barking orders. But from here, above the glass and steel, it's all just silent motion.

Father likes it that way.

"Noise clouds judgment," he once told me. "A ruler must look down and see, not hear."

Tonight, the only sound is the soft hum of the holo-screens and the slow click of his rings against the console as he scrolls.

I stand a step behind him, hands clasped at my back, spine straight. The glass wall stretches from floor to ceiling, reflecting the city in shards of neon—Braxton's bones lit in electric veins.

My reflection is there too.

Black uniform.

Dark eyes.

Expression arranged into calm.

The ghost they talk about.

"Leadership," Father says at last, without looking back, "is not about being liked. Or even understood."

His tone is lazy. Like we've had this conversation a hundred times.

We have.

"It is about control."

"Yes, Father."

He taps the air and one of the holos slides forward, enlarging into a window of smoke and chaos. A raid replay. The date stamp shows yesterday. Outer sectors.

"Pause."

The footage freezes mid-motion.

My breath catches before I can stop it.

A girl in the center of the frame—small, half-obscured by dust—dragging a wounded body with both hands. Her shoulders are braced, her face turned away, but the line of her jaw, the way she leans into the weight, the way she shields the other with her own—

Something in my chest goes cold.

I don't *know* her.

But every instinct says I do.

My fingers twitch. I lock them tighter behind my back.

Father steps closer to the projection, studying it like a specimen.

"Look," he says.

I do. I have to. It's demand of me.

"She is already lost," he goes on, voice clinical. "Her comrade is mortally wounded. Extraction is impossible. Yet she chooses to drag dead weight through a hot zone."

His lips curl, faintly.

"Sentiment. Attachment. A liability dressed up as courage."

My throat feels tight.

To him, they're just pixels on a screen.

"To lead," he says, "you must decide who is worth the air it takes to keep them alive. She has not learned this yet."

The holo throws pale light across his face, hollowing out his features. For a heartbeat, he looks more like a statue than a man. Nothing in him moves except his eyes.

"Your jaw," he notes.

I clamp it shut—too late.

"You disapprove?"

"No, sir."

He turns then, just enough that I see the edge of his smile—not warm, not kind. Something sharper.

"Honesty, Tiberius."

I force my lungs to fill. "It is... inefficient."

"And?"

There's more. He knows it. He will dig until he finds it, even if he has to carve through bone.

"Reckless," I add.

His gaze sharpens. "And?"

My palms are damp. I keep them hidden behind me. "And... it is unnecessary risk for an already lost cause."

He watches me for a long, slow moment.

I keep my face as still as I can.

"You lie badly when it matters most," he says at last.

Heat crawls up my neck.

"It's not a lie," I start—

He cuts me off with a soft click of his tongue.

"Compassion," Dominion says, gesturing back at the frozen girl, "is a crack in the armor. Small. Invisible, at first." He raises a hand. "But once it's there..."

He closes his fist around nothing.

"Pressure does the rest."

The word *pressure* feels very pointed.

He steps close enough that I can feel the cold radiating from the metal in his chest clasp.

"You think I do not see the way you hesitate," he murmurs. "The way you look at the bodies when the reports are finished. The way you listen too long to the screams."

My heartbeat pounds against my ribs. "I follow orders."

"You obey," he agrees. "On the outside." His eyes narrow. "Inside, I am not so sure."

He rests a hand lightly on my shoulder. It might look like a fatherly touch to someone who doesn't know him.

"There is no room for softness in you," he says. "Not if you are to rule after me. Our enemies raise their children on stories of ghosts and monsters. Let them. Fear is useful. But you—"

His fingers tighten, just enough to hurt.

"—you cannot afford to remember that the ghosts are human."

A flash of memory cracks through my skull—

Rain.

Red on blue concrete.

A girl's eyes meeting mine through a storm I created.

I swallow hard enough that it burns.

"I understand," I say.

"Do you?" he asks softly. "Because this—" he nods toward the frozen image of the girl dragging her comrade "—this is what undisciplined hearts produce.

Soldiers who die for sentiment. Leaders who fall for pretty ideals like mercy."

He lets go of my shoulder.

"The Empire does not need your mercy, my son."

The word *son* lands like a weight.

"It needs your certainty."

The silence that follows is suffocating.

"Say it," he orders.

"The Empire needs my certainty," I echo.

"And?"

It's always two layers with him.

"...not my empathy."

"Good." He smiles without warmth. "Then seal the crack before it widens."

He swipes his hand through the holo. The girl disappears into static.

But she's still there, burned behind my eyes.

I shouldn't care.

I don't know her.

I've never met her.

And yet—The shape of her shoulders.

The way she shields the falling.

The way she moves as if she has carried dead weight before and did it anyway—it feels like a ghost brushing past my spine.

Father is already walking toward the door.

"Come, Tiberius. We have a council tonight. The governors will want to see the Ghost Prince at his father's side."

My reflection in the glass watches me turn.

Ghost Prince.

His name—not mine.

I fall into step behind him, boots barely making a sound on the polished floor.

Below us, the city stretches endless, lights blinking like a diagram of veins. Every tower, every alley, every shadow—something I'm expected to control.

And yet, it's the blurred face of a rebel girl in a freeze-frame that keeps replaying when I close my eyes.

Father fears compassion will crack me open.

He's wrong.

The crack is already there.

Hairline.

Quiet.

Growing.

And somewhere out there, in the ruins and smoke and rain, is the reason why.

Chapter 7: The Ash Network

Aly • Age 18

The Undergrid hums like a dying beast.

Cables crawl across the old subway tiles, screens flickering in frantic blues and reds, servers coughing static into the recycled air. This place wasn't built for war, but war found its way into every tunnel anyway.

I've spent the past six hours neck-deep in Empyrium transmissions, decoding purge cycles and cross-mapping survivor routes. It's the only part of the rebellion that feels like saving lives instead of spending them.

"Packet 9G incoming," Vivian calls, sliding a drive toward me. "Try not to vaporize this one."

"It was one time," I say, but my throat feels tight.

A cluster of generals crowds behind me, their voices sharp and eager.

"We release this—"

"—fuel outrage—"

"—finally push Sector Five—"

"—fire up recruitment—"

Not one of them says ***protect the camps***.

A new pair of footsteps enters the argument—lighter, measured. Precise.

Lara Carmichael.

Leader of the rebellion.

My mother.

Everyone snaps straighter.

She studies the map I'm building, the red purge zones, the blinking Nullborn camps clinging to life like sparks in the dark.

"We can use this," General Tovren Ise says to her. "Turn the Empire's brutality into momentum."

Mother's eyes narrow. "Momentum won't save the children in those camps."

Tovren stiffens. "With respect, Commander-General Carmichael—"

"Your respect is irrelevant," she says flatly. "Results are not."

I should feel vindicated.

I don't.

Her gaze shifts to me—sharp, assessing, too knowing.

"Aly," she says, "what would you do with this intel?"

The generals glare.

Vivian pauses mid-keystroke.

I keep my voice steady. "I'd reroute the refugee corridors, warn the camps before the sweeps. Save who we can."

Tovren snorts. "Soft-hearted tactics."

Mother doesn't look away from me. "Soft is not the insult you think it is, General."

But then her eyes harden, just a fraction.

"Still," she adds, quieter, "compassion alone won't win this war. You know that."

I do.

She taught me that herself.

But she also taught me that people matter.

Her voice drops so only I really hear it:

"Don't let your heart blind you, Aly. Use it. Don't let it use you."

It's the closest thing to tenderness she'll allow in public.

Before I can respond—

Vivian taps the console. "Packet open."

Static bursts.

Then: A voice.

Crisp. Cold. Exact.

"Sector Eight sweep: proceed in two teams. Prioritize silence. Remove all Nullborn immediately. Leave no bodies visible."

My breath stops.

That voice.

It unspools through me like wire.

Precision.

Rhythm.

Him.

The same cadence that haunted a rain-soaked ruin years ago.

Not a monster.

A boy.

A blade shaped into a command.

The room leans in.

"Play it again," Tovren demands.

Mother folds her arms. "Let's hear it clearly."

Absolutely not.

If they hear this voice—

hear him—

they'll tear into it, weaponize it, turn him into strategy, propaganda, weakness, target.

And worse—I don't know why, but the idea of them dissecting him makes my skin crawl.

Before Mother can give the order, before anyone can breathe—my fingers move.

I select the packet.

Pull up the command string.

And delete it.

Tovren lunges forward. "What the—?"

"Corrupted file," I lie, tone smooth as glass. "It was unsalvageable."

The system pings confirmation behind me.

Worthless now.

Mother's eyes linger on me for a long, slow moment.

Not angry.

Not confused.

Calculating.

But she says nothing.

Tovren mutters and storms away. Others follow.

I sit very still, hands clasped in my lap because they want to shake.

His voice.

The Empyrium's Ghost.

The unseen commander.

The boy on the beam.

The silhouette in the holo.

It wasn't the rain I remembered.

It was *him*.

And hearing him now—it cuts like a blade pressed gently to my throat.

I close my eyes for one breath.

Two.

Mother's voice drifts to me, low and dangerous as a warning:

"Do not let your heart cost you clarity, Aly."

She walks away.

But clarity is exactly what terrifies me.

I should have kept the packet.

Used it.

Held him up as proof.

But instead—I erased him.

Protected him.

Why?

Because deep down, in a place I refuse to name, I know this:

That voice does not belong to a monster.

It belongs to someone young.

Someone shaped—

not born.

Someone the Empire twisted into a weapon—like they try to do to every Nullborn they steal.

Like they tried to do to me.

"Next packet," Vivian calls.

I inhale, steadying myself, and pull up another report.

I will save who I can.

Even if my mother's own rebellion hates me for it.

Even if the truths in my hands turn to ghosts.

The Ash Network hums around me like a dying heartbeat.

And somewhere in the static—somewhere in the noise—I swear I can still hear his voice.

A ghost whispering orders into a war neither of us chose.

Chapter 8: Grey's Laughter

Tiberius · Age 18

The mess hall at night is the only place on the outpost that feels remotely alive.

Dim blue lights hum overhead, tables half-filled with exhausted soldiers picking apart cold rations. Armor hangs undone. Helmets lie forgotten. Conversation drops to murmurs.

No one here has the energy to pretend.

Except Grey.

Greyson Brantley sits across from me like he owns the table, peeling his ration bar into shreds like he's conducting a science experiment. His eyes flick between the food and me, sharp, curious, always assessing.

He's smart.

Too smart.

Smart enough to know exactly who sits across from him.

"Observation of the night," Grey says, tearing the ration bar in half: "The Empire builds ghosts faster than monuments."

He tosses the piece into his mouth with a grimace.

I raise a brow. "Meaning?"

He points at me with the other half. "Meaning you, Tiberius."

My pulse stills for a fraction of a second.

Grey sees it.

He sees everything.

He smiles anyway—but his eyes flicker with caution, the way someone smiles at a caged animal they trust not to bite.

Most days.

"You realize I'm sitting right here," I say.

"Oh, I do," Grey replies easily. "Trust me, I've never been more aware of a person's proximity in my life."

The words are light.

The fear underneath isn't.

Grey masks it well—in humor, in wit—but I know what fear looks like.

I was raised on it.

I lean back in my chair. "You didn't answer the question."

Grey shrugs. "The Ghost of the Empyrium. Specter. Dominion's son. Half the outpost is convinced you don't sleep, don't bleed, don't blink."

"And you?"

He hesitates—barely—but I catch it.

"I think you're alive. Just... complicated."

I almost laugh, but another part of me waits for a better answer.

The Dominion part.

The part that expects clarity, obedience, certainty.

Grey senses it. His posture shifts—subtle caution.

Then he continues:

"You're not like them," he says. "You're sharper. Quieter. Colder. And every time some officer tells a Specter story, I watch you disappear a little."

It's too honest.

Too close.

"You talk too much," I say, voice flatter than intended.

Grey tenses—for a breath—then forces a grin.

"Well someone has to. You're allergic to words."

I exhale through my nose. "That's not a condition."

"Could've fooled me."

The banter lands, but the air between us stays taut.

Two officers drop into nearby seats, loud and careless.

"Specter cleared a whole corridor with one sweep—"

"—didn't even stop to breathe—"

"—deadliest soldier in the Empire—"

Grey stiffens beside me.

He hates this part.

The legend.

The myth.

The spectacle of death they recite like a bedtime story.

Because he knows the truth:

Their ghost has a pulse.

A hunger.

A leash.

Grey nudges my foot under the table.

Grounding me.

"Hey," he says quietly, "don't disappear on me."

I don't meet his eyes. "I'm not disappearing."

"You are," he insists, soft but firm. "They turn you into a story, and you let them."

My jaw tightens.

A notification pings on the holo-board.

Grey glances up.

OUTER SECTORS—UNUSUAL REBEL COORDINATION DETECTED

The words slam into my chest like a memory.

Rain.

Smoke.

A girl dragging someone through fire.

Eyes like a blade meeting mine across chaos.

I blink hard.

Grey notices instantly.

His voice softens to something close to fear.

"Tiberius. You with me?"

My gaze snaps to him sharply—too sharply.

He flinches.

Just barely.

But enough.

I force the cold out of my voice. "Yes."

He studies me, weighing the risk of pushing further.

He doesn't.

"Good," he murmurs, leaning back to defuse the moment. "Because I swear, if you zone out one more time, I'm filing a report that says Dominion's heir is haunted by tactical boredom."

This time I do laugh—short, sharp, real.

The room quiets.

Soldiers glance over.

Some curious.

Some nervous.

Grey smirks. "Holy shit—

was that an emotion? Quick, someone record history."

I shake my head. "You're insufferable."

"And you're impossible," he shoots back. "We make a great pair."

The warmth of it hits something buried deep in my ribs.

Something that feels dangerously close to trust.

Which is when the feeling dies.

Just like it always does.

I stand abruptly. "I should return to the monitors."

Grey's expression softens, but the shadow of fear returns—the awareness that he is walking a line with me every time he speaks.

"Don't stay locked inside your head," he says. "Even ghosts need air. Even ghosts breathe, Tiberius.

You just forget."

He means well.

He always does.

I nod once—just enough for him to believe it—and step into the corridor.

But behind me, I hear him exhale shakily.

And ahead of me—the memory of rain and a girl whose eyes should've faded by now but haven't follows me like a second shadow.

The crack Dominion fears?

Grey sees it.

And whatever started it in me that night—a blurred face in the rain, a defiant pair of eyes, a ghost I should have forgotten—*it's growing.*

Chapter 9: Kai's Advice

Aly · Age 18

The training mats are still damp with the last round of drills when Mother calls me back to center.

"Again."

Her voice is firm. Not cold.

Never cold.

But it leaves no room for argument.

I lift my hands, settling into stance. My muscles ache from the dawn session; she doesn't comment on the shake in my arms. She never comments on pain—only on form.

"Weight in your back foot," she says, circling me. "Low center. You're too exposed."

I shift. She shakes her head.

"Lower."

I go lower.

Mother steps behind me and gently nudges my ankle outward with her boot. "If your stance fails, your heart fails next. Balance is survival."

Balance.

Lara drills it like a lifeline.

I exhale and strike forward. She sidesteps it easily.

"Predictable," she says. "Again."

I strike again. She blocks, redirects, taps my rib—not to hurt, just to show where a blade would've slipped through.

"Again."

We move across the mats in a pattern we've danced for years—strike, block, pivot, roll.

"Breathe, Aly."

"I am," I gasp.

"No," she says gently. "You're burning the energy you need to think. Slow. Your mind wins fights before your fists do."

I try again, slower this time. She nods.

"Better. But your shoulders are tense. You're bracing for pain before it comes."

"Because it always comes."

Her eyes soften. For a heartbeat, she looks less like a commander and more like the mother who bandaged my scrapes when I was little.

"Yes," she says quietly. "But I will never be the one to teach you through pain."

I swallow hard.

She steps back and gestures. "Again."

We fall into motion.

Precision.

Rhythm.

Breath.

When we break apart, she wipes sweat from her brow with the back of her hand. "You're ready."

"For the strategy meeting?" I ask.

"For what comes next," she corrects. "The men in that room respect your mind, but they'll test your resolve. Don't bend just because you're outnumbered."

"I don't bend," I mutter.

She smiles—faint, but there. "No. You snap. But sometimes that's useful."

A pulse of warmth floods my chest.

It's not praise.

But it's close.

"Come," she says, retrieving her tablet. "Before Tovren works himself into a froth."

I follow her out of the training hall, sweat cooling on my skin, pulse steady but sharp.

Her last words echo in my head:

"***Your mind wins fights before your fists do.***"

Which is exactly what I'll need in the strategy room.

✦ ☽⋆☾ ✦

The moment we step inside, the noise hits like a wave.

General Tovren is pacing with the energy of a man itching for a fight he hasn't yet been given. Two more generals argue across the holo-table, their voices overlapping until they're just static.

Holo-maps flicker above us—supply routes, Empyrium choke points, Nullborn camp markers scattered like fragile stars.

Kai Virel stands at the far end of the table, arms folded, expression patient in the way only brilliant men and predators master. His eyes flick briefly to me, then to Mother, then to the table.

He's been waiting.

Mother steps forward. "Report."

Tovren slams a hand onto the holo. "We hit Sector Five with a full offensive. Firestorm tactics. Broadcast it. Show the Empire we're not afraid."

"We *are* afraid," Kai says dryly. "That's how we stay alive."

Tovren rounds on him. "Patience won't win a war!"

"And ego will lose it," Kai replies.

His tone is quiet, steady, cutting.

Mother lifts a hand before the argument escalates. "We consider all options."

I take a breath and step forward. "We have six Nullborn camps still exposed. If we divert power from the grid here—" I swipe my hand across the holo, routes shifting, "—we buy them time. Two weeks at least. Enough for relocation."

Tovren scoffs. "You want us to save scraps while the Empire razes entire sectors?"

Kai tilts his head. "Scraps grow into armies. Corpses grow into nothing."

Mother hides a smile behind her hand.

I push on. "A full strike is suicide. But a surgical hit buys lives. And the Empire won't see us coming."

Tovren throws his hands up. "You're both obsessed with shadows and stealth—"

"Because shadows and stealth work," Kai interrupts, gaze cutting to me. "Aly understands that."

Mother raises a brow—quietly proud.

Tovren glares at both of us. "So what then? We whisper in the dark forever?"

"No," Kai says. "We choose our battles. We strike where they never expect. Not because we're weak—but because we're not careless."

Silence firms around his words.

Mother nods once. "Proceed with Kai's plan. Aly will refine the intel."

Tovren curses but doesn't push the issue.

Then the holo-table flickers, shifting to a new list—upcoming neutral training exhibitions. Fighters listed under aliases.

Names scroll by:

Iron Wolf.

Wraithline.

Solace-2

Echo-9.

And then—

Specter.

The room tilts.

My breath stutters.

Mother notices the shift. "Aly?"

"Fine," I choke out. "Just—surprised they're sending high-level operatives."

Kai's gaze sharpens. "You reacted to that one. Why?"

I swallow. Hard.

"Just a codename," I whisper.

"Is it?" Kai asks gently.

I look away. "We should focus on the camps."

Kai watches me with a quiet, knowing patience that makes something in my chest twist.

"Specter," he murmurs. "Empire's myth. Dominion's knife."

Tovren snorts. "Probably just propaganda to scare us."

No.

I know better.

I remember rain.

I remember chaos.

I remember a silhouette commanding death like he was born to it.

Mother steps forward, tone clipped. "Leave the exhibition list for now. Our priority is survival, not sport."

The generals disperse.

Kai lingers.

Mother's gaze follows me.

"You did well," Lara says softly. "But you were shaken."

"I'm fine."

"No." She steps closer, voice lowering. "You're guarded. Find the source of your fear, Aly. Or it will find you."

Her thumb brushes my shoulder once—warmth through armor—before she walks away.

The words eat at me long after she's gone.

I return to the comm hall to file intel. The hum of servers fills the room.

Then every monitor flickers.

Static crackles.

A crimson sigil floods the Undergrid comms.

The Empire crest. A public broadcast.

That never happens.

People freeze, confused, wary.

A voice booms:

"*Announcing the Empyrium entrant for the Neutral Exhibition:*

ELITE UNIT—SPECTER."

My heart slams into my ribs.

A figure appears:

Black armor.

Full mask.

Every line designed to hide identity.

Whispers erupt:

"Why the mask?"

"Empire hiding something?"

"No face? That's new."

"They're protecting him."

Of course they are.

Everyone in the Empyrium knows what the Tyrant's son looks like.

They can't risk him being recognized.

This... anonymity?

This uniform?

It's camouflage.

A lie.

A way to let Specter fight without revealing the truth.

Kai appears beside me, scanning the feed. "They're guarding him.

Interesting."

I barely hear him.

Because the way the figure moves—poised, precise, predatory—matches a rhythm burned into my bones.

Rain.

A collapsed warehouse.

A pair of eyes above me. A voice ordering death.

The broadcast ends.

Silence floods the hall.

And I know, with terrifying clarity:

Kai turns toward me slowly. "Aly—"

"I'm entering," I say—

and the truth lands like a blade.

His inhale is sharp. "Because of Specter?"

"Because it's necessary."

He watches me with that calm, assessing intelligence I've always trusted.

And nods once.

No judgment. No surprise.

He already knew.

I step away from the monitors, pulse hammering.

My mother's voice echoes behind my ribs:

Find the source of your fear.

I've found it.

He wears a mask now.

But I know him.

Specter.

The Empire's phantom.

The boy in the rain.

The silence that follows presses against my ears like a weight.

Footsteps echo behind me—steady, clipped.

Mother.

Her presence hits the room before her voice does. "What happened?"

Kai gestures to the frozen screens. "The Empire is entering Specter into the Exhibition."

Mother's jaw tightens. "Of course they are." A pause. "To show dominance without starting a war."

Or to hide their son in plain sight.

My stomach churns.

Kai turns to me, measuring. "Aly has... thoughts about entering."

Mother whirls toward me. "Absolutely not."

The words hit like a slap—sharp, instinctive.

I lift my chin. "I didn't say anything yet."

"You didn't need to." Her eyes are already burning into mine. "I know that look. That spark. It means you've already made a decision. And I'm telling you now—no."

Her voice is command.

Her fear is mother.

"Lara—" Kai starts.

She cuts him off. "She is my daughter. And Specter is lethal."

The room goes still.

Mother steps closer, lowering her voice so only I can hear. "You think I don't see you, Aly? You've been distracted for weeks. Unsettled. Haunted. I sent you to find the source of your fear—not walk into its hands."

My throat tightens. "This is where I find it."

"This is where you die," she snaps.

Kai steps forward carefully. "Lara. The Exhibition is regulated. No lethal rounds. No free kills. And Aly's instincts are—"

"This isn't about instincts," Mother says fiercely. "This is about her stepping into a ring with the Empire's most dangerous weapon."

"And knowing how that weapon moves may save thousands," Kai counters.

Mother rounds on him. "Don't you dare reduce her to strategy."

"I'm not," he says evenly. "I'm stating a truth."

She breathes hard once, twice, her glare shifting between the two of us.

Finally she turns back to me, voice low and trembling with a kind of fear she's never shown in public.

"Aly... I can't lose you. Not to a mask. Not to that tyrant and his games."

I swallow around the ache in my chest. "You won't."

"You don't know that."

"Yes," I whisper. "I do."

Her breath catches.

And suddenly she sees it.

Not recklessness.

Not bravado.

Resolve.

The same resolve she trained into me.

The same resolve she's lived by her whole life.

Mother closes her eyes. One hand drifts to my cheek—not commanding, not correcting. Simply holding.

Finally, she exhales. "If you enter... you will not go unprepared."

"I won't," I promise.

She steps back with visible reluctance. "This isn't permission. It's acceptance."

And then—so soft only I hear it:

"Please...

come back to me."

My chest cracks.

I nod.

Her shoulders sag, just a fraction. Then she straightens herself back into Commander-General Carmichael.

"You'll have one night to prepare," she says. "Kai, get her the footage. Aly, gather your gear."

Kai nods sharply. "Already doing it."

Mother hesitates in the doorway, eyes catching on me once more. Fear. Pride. Love. All of it burning.

Then she leaves.

The silence closes in behind her.

I stand alone in the dim hall, the echo of Specter's masked silhouette flickering in the dark screens.

I whisper the truth to myself:

"***If I don't face this ghost now, I'll meet him on a battlefield I can't control.***"

And for the first time, the fear doesn't chase me.

I chase it.

Chapter 10: Arena Ghosts

Tiberius - Specter

The Neutral Exhibition

Round One:

Specter vs Iron Wolf

The roar of the crowd hits before the lights do.

Sound first—a low, hungry rumble rolling through the arena like distant thunder—then the glare of white spotlights crashing down over polished steel.

I step out into it.

The mask seals with a soft hiss against my jaw.

Filters hum.

HUD lines blink to life across my vision.

ION CROWN ENTRANT: SPECTER

The announcer's voice booms overhead, theatrically distorted.

"Representing the Empyrium—the Empire's elite unit—SPECTER!"

The noise spikes. Some cheer. Some jeer. It doesn't matter. Specter exists for them.

Tiberius exists for Dominion.

My boots strike the arena floor with even, measured steps as I cross to my mark.

My opponent is already there.

CALLSIGN: IRON WOLF

Broad shoulders. Heavy armor etched with crude fang patterns. He rolls his neck like he can intimidate me through flexing alone.

He can't see my face behind the mask, but still, he points a blade at me.

"Try to keep it interesting, ghost," he says, voice tinny through his helmet filter.

The bell cracks through the air.

He charges.

I don't.

I shift one step to the side, let his momentum barrel past, then pivot. A quick hook of my boot behind his ankle sends him crashing to one knee. The crowd reacts, a ripple of sound.

He recovers faster than I expect.

Good.

He swings his training blade at my ribs. I catch his wrist, redirect, slam the flat of my staff into his chest plate.

Point.

The tally flashes on the holo: **SPECTER – 1**.

Iron Wolf snarls and comes again—heavy, aggressive, predictable. I let him wear himself out. Redirect. Step aside. Let him overextend. Tap the gaps in his stance.

Another point.

And another.

The final exchange is almost boring.

He tries a desperate overhead strike. I sidestep, sweep his legs, and hold my blade at the notch of his throat guard until the bell snaps again.

"Match—SPECTER!"

The crowd erupts.

I don't raise my blade. I don't bow. I turn away.

Iron Wolf slams a fist against the floor, more embarrassed than injured.

I should feel triumphant. Or at least satisfied.

I feel... nothing.

Then movement flickers at the edge of my HUD on a neighboring platform.

Another match beginning.

A figure steps into the opposite arena ring—slighter, leaner, stance low and balanced. Helmet on, visor dark, armor matte and clean.

CALLSIGN: RIVEN flashes over her in pale white.

I don't register why my chest tightens.

I just watch.

✦ ☽⋆☾ ✦

Aly - Riven

Riven vs Solace-2

The spotlights are hotter than I expected.

They burn down through the haze of dust and recycled air, turning the arena into a silver bowl, all edges and echoes. My helmet amplifies my breath, each inhale a metallic ghost against my ears.

OUTER COLONIES ENTRANT: RIVEN

The announcer milks it, stretching out the name like a dare to the Empire.

Across from me, my opponent—Solace-2—rolls his shoulders and dips his visor in a slow, respectful nod. His armor is lighter than mine, more flexible, built for speed.

Good. I like fighting people who think they can outrun their problems.

The bell sounds.

He moves first—smooth, deliberate, a testing strike aimed at my right shoulder.

I block. Hard. The impact jolts up my arm.

Not bad.

We circle each other. His footwork is clean, but it's a pattern. I've spent years reading patterns—supply routes, patrol shifts, execution schedules, the way a man's hand trembles before he pulls a trigger.

He feints low, comes high.

This time I'm already there.

Steel glances against steel, sparks snapping between us. I step inside his guard and tap the sensor node over his heart.

Point.

The crowd reacts with a sharp cheer. My pulse answers, steady, not spiking. I back off, reset my stance, breath sawing slow and controlled.

He grins under his mask. "Not bad, Colonies."

"Likewise," I say.

He comes in again, faster, sharper. We trade blows—three, four, five in rapid succession. I feel the strain in my arms.

Solace-2 commits to a high spin.

Mistake.

I sweep his leg mid-turn, send him off-balance, then drive my blade lightly but decisively into his chest plate, right over the core.

The bell shrieks.

"Match—RIVEN!"

The crowd roars louder this time. I straighten, chest heaving—not from exhaustion, but from the weight of being here. In the open. In front of them.

In front of him.

Because I feel it—

That prickle at the back of my neck.

The cold, aware stare.

I turn my head slightly, pretending to scan the stands, but my gaze catches on a dark figure at the edge of a neighboring platform.

Black armor.

Unmoving.

Watching.

Specter.

Even at this distance, his stillness feels like a hand around my throat.

I force myself to look away first.

The exit tunnel yawns ahead. I step into shadow, pulse thrumming.

This was just the first match.

He's waiting at the end of all of them.

Tiberius

Round Two: Specter vs Wraithline

By the time I step into the arena for the second round, the noise has become a living thing.

It climbs the walls, rattles the rails, vibrates faintly through the floor.

MATCH: SPECTER vs WRAITHLINE

Wraithline is leaner than Iron Wolf, armor streaked with paint to mimic motion blur—like he's already running. Two crackling shock-blades hum at his hips.

He salutes lazily. "Big fan of your work, Specter," he purrs over the comm. "Mind giving me a slow death so I can enjoy it?"

My grip tightens on my staff.

"No."

The bell snaps and he's on me.

He's fast. Faster than Iron Wolf by a long shot. He uses reach, momentum, angles. His blades dart in from unexpected directions—

—but Dominion trained me against a hundred styles. Against men who were faster, stronger, smarter than this.

I parry. One. Two. Three. Staff sliding along the crackling blades, redirecting rather than absorbing.

My HUD tracks his patterns.

My mind doesn't.

Because above the clash, over his snarled curses, my attention keeps snagging on the far arena.

Riven.

She's on the lower platform now, waiting, helmet tilted down, shoulders rolling like she's resetting her muscles.

Wraithline lunges for my throat.

I knock his arm away at the last possible second.

He laughs, breathless. "Thought I almost had you there, Ghost."

"You didn't."

I drive a knee into his sternum, then spin, sweeping his legs. He twists, catches himself on one hand, kicks off the floor, and nearly clips my head.

Nearly.

I grab his ankle mid-air, yank, and slam him flat on his back.

Blade to his chest.

The bell screams.

"Match—SPECTER!"

He wheezes out a chuckle. "Hells. No wonder they keep your face hidden."

I don't answer.

Because my gaze is already drifting past him—

—to where the holo-board is shifting, announcing the wild card round.

WILD CARD: RIVEN vs ECHO-9

Echo-9.

The one who fought Wraithline and lost, but still the one didn't stay down.

Riven steps onto that platform.

Something in my chest drops like a stone.

✦ ☽⋆☾ ✦

Aly

Wild Card Round: Riven vs Echo-9

I wasn't supposed to be back in the ring this fast.

My arms are still humming from Solace-2. My ribs ache from old bruises. Sweat clings under the lining of my helmet, itching where I can't scratch.

But the board flashes:

WILD CARD ROUND: RIVEN vs ECHO-9

And Command chose my name.

Of course they did.

Echo-9 stalks out from his tunnel like he owns the arena.

His armor is scarred from his last match, fresh weld seams, a dent across one pauldron he either couldn't or wouldn't have repaired. He carries a shock-staff and a knife, both blunt-edged but brutal.

He rolls his head, bones popping loud enough I hear it through the air.

He wants this.

The bell slams through the arena.

He hits me like a battering ram.

There's no feeling-out. No cautious first exchange. His staff crashes into my guard with enough force to knock me two steps back. My boots squeal against the floor, rubber scraping steel.

Pain punches through my left side, a flare beneath my ribs.

I choke on a breath.

My knee nearly buckles, and something hot lances up my side—a reminder that pain keeps score even when the crowd doesn't.

He laughs—a harsh, hissing sound. "On your feet, little ghost."

I don't answer.

I don't have the air.

He comes in again, relentless. His style is ugly and efficient, less art, more survival. I recognize the flavor of it. He's fought in dirt pits, back alleys, places where losing meant losing more than a match.

I've fought there too. Just with different walls.

He feints high, slams low, the staff cracking against my thigh. My knee buckles. The crowd roars with every hit he lands, the sound folding over itself until it's not cheers, it's waves.

"NINE! NINE! NINE!"

He swings for my head.

I drop under it by instinct more than thought, feeling the whisper of wind as the staff passes over where my neck had been.

If this weren't regulated—if there were no safeties—I'd be dead twice over already.

My lungs burn.

The world narrows to three things:

The ache in my ribs, the weight of my blade, and the knowledge that

Specter is somewhere above, watching

I force my legs to move.

He lunges. I let him get close this time, too close, feel the heat off his armor as he overcommits. I catch his wrist, twist, step in under his guard.

Our helmets nearly slam together.

I drive my knee into his thigh.

He grunts.

Again.

He snarls, trying to wrench free.

I hold on like I'm drowning, pivot, and rip the staff from his hand. It clatters across the floor.

The crowd flips, half booing, half screaming.

He doesn't hesitate—goes for the knife at his hip.

I knock his arm aside and slam the flat of my blade into his chest node, shoulders shaking from the effort.

Clear, decisive contact.

The bell splits the air.

"Match—RIVEN!"

My victory flashes, pale and unreal.

My body doesn't believe it.

Echo-9 huffs out a breath and drops to his back, chest heaving. The fight drains out of him all at once, like someone unplugged him.

I'm panting hard as I take a step back—and my leg almost gives.

The world tilts. I catch myself at the last second, drawing in a ragged breath that tastes like metal and recycled air.

For a moment, I can't hear the crowd.

Can't hear the announcer.

Can't hear anything except my own pulse slamming in my ears.

Then—a pinprick feeling.

Like a laser sight between my shoulder blades.

I lift my head.

Across the arena, on the upper platform, Specter stands at the rail, dark armor framed in light. I can't see his face, but his helmet is angled directly at me.

At my eyes.

Through the layers of metal and glass and air, something inside me recognizes him—and recognizes that he recognizes me back.

I turn away first.

If I don't, I'm not sure I'll be able to walk.

Tiberius

The wild card round wasn't supposed to matter.

It was filler. A concession to sponsors and odds-makers. A second chance for Echo-9, the crowd favorite, to claw his way back into the narrative.

Then Riven stepped into the ring.

And now I can't breathe properly.

Echo-9 hits her hard enough on the first exchange to make the floor vibrate under my boots.

Grey leans on the rail beside me. "That's a concussion waiting to happen," he mutters.

I say nothing.

Because she's getting up.

Slowly. Painfully. One hand braced on her thigh, the other wrapped around her blade so tight her knuckles—what little I can see of them under the gloves—must be white.

She shouldn't rise.

She does.

Echo-9 slams into her again.

And again.

Every time she hits the floor, the crowd chants his number.

Every time she stands, something tightens in my chest.

My hands curl on the rail so hard the metal protests.

"You're gripping like you want to jump in there," Grey says quietly. "Which is insane, by the way."

I know it's insane.

I know I'm Specter.

I know she's a rebel.

I know the logical thing would be to hope Echo-9 breaks her so I don't have to face her at full strength.

But when he swings for her head and she barely ducks in time—my heart misses a beat.

She counterattacks, body moving on borrowed energy and something sharper. Desperation. Will. The refusal to stay down.

I've seen that will before.

In a warehouse. In the rain.

When she finally disarms Echo-9 and slams her blade into his chest sensor, it isn't a flourish. It's a last act of defiance from someone who has nothing left.

Grey whistles.

"If she wasn't your opponent, I'd be rooting for her."

My throat tightens.

Echo-9 falls.

She sways on her feet.

Just barely stays upright.

The bell shrieks: "Match—RIVEN!"

The crowd erupts.

But I don't hear it.

I'm staring at the way she tries to walk off the platform and nearly buckles on the first step.

"She's hurt," I say before I can stop myself.

Grey turns, studies her, then me. "So are half the people down there."

"Not like that."

The board shifts.

FINAL MATCH: SPECTER vs RIVEN

Grey whistles softly. "Well. That's... poetic."

My pulse slams once, hard enough that my vision tightens at the edges.

Because the girl who refused to die in the warehouse—the girl who just refused to fall in front of thousands—is walking straight toward me.

And for the first time in my life, I'm not entirely sure I want to win.

Tiberius

FINAL MATCH

The lights feel hotter for the final match.

Or maybe it's just me.

My armor has cooled, but my skin feels too tight beneath it, every nerve drawn thin. The arena floor gleams beneath my boots as I walk to center ring.

FINAL MATCH: SPECTER vs RIVEN

Across from me, she appears through the tunnel—

Riven.

Her armor is darker up close, matte plating scarred with fresh impact marks from Echo-9. Her helmet covers everything but the faint gleam of eyes behind a narrow visor, barely visible unless you're this close.

We are this close.

She moves like she's trying very hard not to show she's in pain.

The announcer milks the moment.

"On this side, the Empire's ghost—the Ion Crown's blade—SPECTER!"

The crowd roars.

"And opposing him, the Colonies' rising phantom—a storm that refuses to break—RIVEN!"

More cheering. More chanting. Names thrown like sparks.

I hear none of it.

Because the second she looks up at me, the arena falls away.

It's her.

Not just in rhythm now. Not just in suspicion.

It's the girl from the warehouse.

The girl who dragged her dead through smoke and stared up at me like I was the monster under the bed.

That stare hits me again, through layers of metal and years and lies.

The bell goes off like a gunshot.

We move.

✦ ☽⋆☾ ✦

Aly

The world outside my helmet collapses into shapes and light.

Specter stands at the center of the arena, black against the glare. Up close, he's taller than I expected—presence heavy, like gravity has quietly decided he matters more than anyone else in the room.

I hate that I notice that.

I hate that my chest tightens.

The announcer's voice becomes a distant echo. My focus narrows to three things:

His stance—balanced, efficient.

His hands—relaxed, deadly.

His stillness—not calm, but *contained violence.*

The bell sounds.

I move on instinct.

I dart right, testing his guard. He doesn't overcommit. He meets me halfway, staff snapping up to knock aside my first strike.

The impact jolts through me—not fear.

Recognition.

His movements are precise, not flashy.

Predictable—but only if you know the pattern.

And I do.

I duck under his arm, reaching for the edge of his mask, desperate to confirm the truth I've carried for two years.

He deflects me effortlessly.

He's holding back.

Why?

Specter doesn't hold back.

The Ghost of the Empyrium doesn't hold back.

But this soldier—this masked phantom—hesitates for a breath.

One heartbeat.

Exactly like he did before he let me live.

Exactly like the rain.

We clash again—shoulder-to-shoulder, palms sliding, bodies locking into a rhythm that feels less like combat and too much like a dance.

I hate how natural it is.

I hate how my body knows the rhythm of someone who ruined my life.

I hate—

that I don't want to stop.

He's strong.

But that isn't what makes something inside me flinch.

It's ***how he moves.***

Minimal. No wasted motion. Every step a choice, not a reaction.

Just like in the warehouse.

Just like on the beam.

Just like under the rain.

I force myself forward—a flurry of strikes: high, low, feint, pivot. Because if I let myself think, if I let myself feel, I'll freeze.

He doesn't answer with aggression.

He answers with precision.

Redirect. Deflect. Guide.

Like he's fighting with me.

Like he knows the steps.

He's holding back.

Why?

Tiberius

Riven fights like she has something to prove and no energy left to prove it.

Her strikes are fast, clever, adaptive. She reads me the way I'm used to reading others, changing tempo the moment she feels resistance.

She sweeps low.

I jump, barely clearing the arc.

She recovers from the miss faster than she should, spinning with the momentum, blade coming up toward my ribs.

I deflect with the staff.

Our forearms collide—bone, impact, heat.

The jolt stings.

She doesn't back away.

For a heartbeat, we're locked—

arm to arm, breath to breath,

visors nearly touching.

And through the narrow slit in her mask...

I see her eyes.

Indigo blue.

Not pale.

Not cold.

But deep—so deep it's like falling.

Furious.

Alive.

Bright enough to cut through the floodlights and the noise and every layer of armor I'm wearing.

They shouldn't be that visible.

They shouldn't be that familiar.

They shouldn't hit me this hard.

My pulse spikes.

Something in my chest stumbles, misfires.

Those eyes—

The same ones staring at me through rain and ruin.

The same ones that refused to die when everything around her did.

Indigo like lightning swallowed by night.

And they ask me—silently, devastatingly:

Why?

Why did you let me live?

Why didn't you finish it?

Why are you hesitating now?

Why do you look at me like you know me?

I tear my gaze away first.

I shouldn't feel anything.

I ***can't*** feel anything.

But those eyes—

they're a weapon I have no defense against.

I tear my gaze away first.

I shouldn't feel anything.

I ***can't*** feel anything.

But those eyes—

they're a weapon I have no defense against.

I push her back, more gently than I should.

She stumbles, catches herself, then snarls something wordless and comes at me again.

The crowd is losing its mind. I hear my name and hers chanted like opposing spells.

"SPEC-TER!"

"RIV-EN!"

We trade blows—fast now, faster—our bodies falling into a rhythm that feels disturbingly natural.

Too natural.

Because I know where she's going to step next.
And she knows where I'm going to block.
We're not just fighting.
We're... syncing.
And I don't know what to do with that.
She feints left.
I match.
She changes direction mid-stride.
Smart.
I step back, narrowing my stance—a small tell I never give opponents.
She notices.
Of course she does.
She presses.
A flurry of strikes—precise, surgical.
Her hands tremble only when she breathes in, not out.
Fear suppressed.
Rage contained.
Purpose burning.
I parry, redirect, block.
And then—

She lands a palm strike against my chest plate hard enough to knock me back two steps.

My heart stutters.
Not from the hit.
From the realization:
I know this girl.
I know her fight.
I know her courage.
I know her scream from the rain.
It slams into me with brutal clarity.
The mask hides my face, but she sees the hesitation anyway.
She stops.
Just for a fraction.
Her eyes widen.
She knows.

She *knows*.

✦ ☽⋆☾ ✦

Aly

The impact of my palm strike reverberates up my arm—sharp, jarring—but what truly knocks the breath from me is how he reacts:

He stumbles.

Not dramatically.

Not sloppily.

Just—***unprepared.***

Specter is never unprepared.

And the way he regains balance—

that shift of weight,

that precise correction,

those angles—

It's him.

It's him.

Specter.

The Ghost of the Empyrium.

The Tyrant's son.

The boy on the beam.

Every piece snaps into place like gears locking into a weapon.

I freeze.

Just long enough for him to see it.

My confirmation.

His guilt.

Our truth.

The world tilts.

He should be trying to crush me.

Specter. The Empire's ghost. Dominion's heir.

Instead, he redirects.

He shifts.

He catches my strikes and *turns them aside* instead of driving them back into me.

It's infuriating.

It's terrifying.

It's familiar.

Every time our weapons collide, there's that half-second of guidance in his touch—the subtle steering, the redirection that keeps me from taking the worst of the blow.

Like he's protecting me.

I don't want his protection.

I want ***answers***.

I push harder, ignoring the screaming in my ribs. My breathing slips off rhythm. My vision pulses at the edges.

He notices.

Of course he does.

He eases up.

I see it—

that micro-hesitation,

that fractional slackening of force,

that moment where he chooses not to hurt me.

Rage snaps through me like a whip. I compensate with a brutal overhead strike. He blocks—and ***this time*** I feel his full strength behind the staff.

My grip falters.

His doesn't.

Our weapons lock above our heads.

"Why didn't you kill me?" I hiss, so low only his helmet audio could possibly catch it.

It's reckless.

Self-destructive.

Too raw.

But it tears itself out of me anyway.

He goes still.

Completely.

For one impossible beat, the fight stops.

The crowd keeps screaming, oblivious.

His answer is barely a breath.

"...I don't know."

Something inside me cracks.

His hand slides along my forearm in a block—and instead of pushing me back, he *guides* my movement, redirecting it into something gentler.

What the hell is he doing?

Why is he—

Why am I—

We move like magnets in a storm.

Opposite charges drawn into a single current.

My pulse is a war drum.

My breath is smoke.

My hatred is shaking.

Specter ducks under my strike, spins behind me—I don't strike backward even though I should.

He doesn't attack even though he could.

We both hesitate.

At the same time.

A mirrored, terrifying, perfect pause.

And in that heartbeat—I feel exactly what he feels:

I should kill you.

I can't.

Tiberius

The question hits like a shock-rod to the spine.

Why didn't you kill me?

Because I wasn't supposed to hesitate.

Because Dominion trained hesitation out of me.

Because that day in the warehouse should've ended with no survivors.

Because something in me refused.

I don't have a word for that something.

The admission scrapes my throat on the way out.

"I don't know."

Her eyes flare—pain? Fury? Accusation?

Or something worse.

Something that mirrors me.

There's a rule in the Exhibition:

NO removing masks.

So I don't.

But every part of me wants to.

To see if the girl inside this armor matches the memory of the girl in the rain.

To see if I imagined her.

To see if she's real.

She wrenches her blade free and charges again, but there's a tremor in her shoulders that wasn't there before.

Not weakness.

Emotion.

It mirrors the shake in my hands.

The referee's voice cuts faintly through the noise:

"***Thirty seconds***!"

We move.

Harder. Faster. Desperate.

She strikes for my side. I twist, let the blade skim my armor, and hook her wrist, turning her momentum into a spin she barely catches. She drops low, sweeps for my legs—

I jump.

We collide mid-air, crash down, roll across the polished steel.

For a heartbeat, our helmets nearly slam together.

I feel her breath vibrate against my filter.

I feel mine echo back at her.

We freeze again.

Neither of us takes the opening.

Neither of us deals the finishing blow.

We both hesitate.

The bell shrieks.

"**MATCH—DRAW**!"

The arena erupts.

A draw.

No victor.

No loser.

Just two ghosts circling each other in the wreckage of a fight neither of us could finish.

Riven pushes to her feet, legs shaking.

I rise more steadily—but only because I've perfected the art of standing when everything inside me is collapsing.

We stare at each other.

She knows.

That I'm Specter.

That I'm the Ghost of the Empyrium.

That I'm the boy on the beam.

And I know.

She's the girl from the rain.

The girl who shouldn't have survived me.

The girl who keeps surviving anyway.

I should say something.

Anything.

I don't.

She doesn't turns away this time, helmet dipping down, body rigid as she steps back.

The crowd chants both our names.

It sounds like a promise.

Or a threat.

Or something far more dangerous than either.

✦ ☽⋆☾ ✦

Aly

The announcer shouts something about diplomatic victory.

Crowd roaring. Lights flashing. Names chanted like gospel.

I hear none of it.

Because Specter steps back—

just one step—

and **hesitates**.

Hesitates.

No soldier hesitates.

No Empyrium elite hesitates.

Specter never hesitates.

Except him.

Except the boy in the rain.

Except the Tyrant's son who looked down at me through smoke and ruin

and *chose* not to kill me.
My pulse hammers against my ribs.
He turns—
just enough for me to see the muscles in his jaw shift beneath the mask,
just enough to see the rigid control in his shoulders falter,
just enough to know he isn't breathing right,
just enough to know this wasn't a performance
or a duty
or a clean Empyrium show match.
This was **recognition**.
And the way he leaves the arena—
slow,
measured,
almost steady,
but not steady enough—
tells me one thing:
He knows exactly who I am too.

Tiberius

The door seals behind me with a hydraulic hiss.
For a moment, the sound is too loud.
Too sharp.
Like the arena followed me inside and is still rattling around under my ribs.
My hands won't stop shaking as I unclip my helmet.
The pressure release hisses softly.
Cool air hits my face, but my skin is burning.
I catch my reflection in the polished locker wall—
pale eyes, sweat-damp hair, jaw locked so tight it aches.
"What the hell was that," I whisper.
The helmet creaks under my grip.
Her eyes won't leave my mind.
The fury.
The recognition.
The question.
Why didn't you kill me?

I drag a hand down my face.

I don't know.

I don't know.

I—

The door slams open.

"Okay," Grey says as he steps in and lets it reseal behind him. "You're either about to pass out, punch a wall, or spontaneously combust. Which should I prep for?"

I don't answer.

His gaze drops to my hands—to the faint tremor, to the helmet I'm holding like it's the only thing keeping me anchored.

"Tiberius," he says, humor gone.

I stare past him.

He steps closer, cautious, like I'm an exposed wire. "You fought like your brain was running two different programs out there. Who was she?"

My pulse spikes.

He sees it. Of course he does.

"Oh fuck," Grey breathes. "You *know* her."

My grip tightens. "I don't."

The lie tastes like metal.

"Bullshit," he says flatly. "You hesitated twice. You pulled half your blows. You let the match end in a draw."

"It was regulated sparring," I snap.

"You don't spar," Grey shoots back. "You execute."

My jaw clamps shut.

He studies me—not like a subordinate looking at Dominion's son, but like a friend trying to see through armor.

"Tiberius," he says quietly, "what happened?"

A breath tears out of me, shallow and ragged.

"I've seen her before."

"When?"

The memory slams through me:

Rain like needles.

Collapsed beams.

A girl covered in blood and grief, refusing to fall.

Her eyes locking on mine while death swarmed around her.

"The warehouse," I say. "Two years ago. The raid. She was there."

Grey goes very still.

"The one from the intel packet?" he asks. "The girl who lived?"

"Yes."

"And she was in the arena today."

"Yes."

"Masked."

"Yes."

"And you recognized her anyway."

I swallow. "...Yes."

Grey sinks onto the bench like his legs gave out. "Oh, that's bad."

I glare. "Insightful."

He glares back—then softens. "What did you recognize? You couldn't see her face."

I stare down at my unsteady hands.

"...the way she moved."

"Her form?"

"No."

A shake of my head.

"Her rhythm."

Grey's eyes widen.

Because he understands:

I don't recognize people.

Dominion trained it out of me.

Faces blur.

Names vanish.

Everything reduces to threat or non-threat.

I shouldn't have space for... rhythm.

Except hers.

"She kept getting up," I say softly. "Echo-9 hit her hard enough to break most soldiers. She stood anyway."

"That's what bothers you?"

"No." My throat tightens. "Yes. It's... all of it. Shut up."

Grey drags a hand through his hair. "Dominion can never know."

The room seems to drop ten degrees.

He's right.

If Dominion finds out I hesitated—

that I recognized an enemy—

that I spared her, twice—

that I'm thinking about her now—

He'll carve the weakness out of me.

One way or another.

Grey looks up. "Did she hesitate too?"

The question lands like a blade.

In the arena—

with her body pressed against mine—

with her blade poised—

I *felt* it.

The opening she didn't take.

"Yes," I say.

Grey exhales hard. "Great. Perfect. Fantastic. You've trauma-bonded with a rebel who wants you dead."

"I told you to shut up," I mutter.

"And I told you I'm the only one who'll say this to your face," he fires back. Then, softer: "Whatever that was out there? You bury it. No one sees it. Not the officers. Not Command. Definitely not Dominion. You bury this deep. You're both lucky those masks stayed on."

I don't argue.

Because he's right.

If the Empire knew Specter recognized a rebel?

If the Colonies knew Riven hesitated?

We'd both be dead before sunrise.

"You act like she was just another opponent," Grey says.

"She wasn't," I say.

"I know," he replies. "That's the problem."

Silence drops between us.

Grey steps closer, resting a careful hand on my shoulder—like he's not sure if I'll let him.

"What is she to you?" he asks quietly.

The answer drags itself out of me.

"...a loose end."

Grey scoffs. "Bullshit. Try again."

I flinch.

He doesn't let up.

"You're shaken because she lived. And because when she looked at you, you didn't see fear. You saw recognition. Maybe even—" he hesitates "—understanding. Some part of you doesn't know if you're supposed to destroy her, follow her, or ask her what the hell she did to you in the rain."

My throat burns.

Grey holds my gaze.

"Tiberius," he says softly,

"the girl in the arena isn't just a ghost.

She's the one haunting you.

And if you don't control that?

It's going to control you."

My fingers tighten around the helmet.

Because he's right.

And because, deep down, in a place I don't let Dominion touch—

it already has.

Chapter 11: Mirror City

Tiberius

From up here, the city doesn't look real.

The balcony juts out from the side of the Braxton Palace like a blade angled over Empyrium's throat. Wind drags across my face—humid, metallic, thick with storm-oil from the upper turbines. The scent settles in the back of my mouth, bitter as copper.

Below, the neon grid bleeds color into the darkness, stretching farther than my eyes can follow. Currents of blue, violet, and that harsh Dominion-red pulse in time with the transport lines. Every light feels sharp. Every shadow feels watched.

Every breath feels like a mistake.

I curl my fingers around the railing until my knuckles whiten. The metal bites back, cold and unforgiving—unlike the heat that keeps rising beneath my skin.

The metal bites down, cold enough to steady me for half a breath—before heat claws its way back under my skin.

I should be downstairs in the strategy hall.

I should be standing in front of Dominion and answering the one question he keeps repeating:

Why did you hesitate?

He didn't say the rest, but I heard it anyway.

Why didn't you finish her?

My stomach twists. I force a slow inhale, but the air feels too heavy, like the storm is sitting on my lungs. The sky roils overhead—clouds dark and churning, rimmed with bruised light.

I blink, and for a moment the arena flashes behind my eyes.

The clang of metal.

The shudder of each impact up my arm.

Her breath catching as our blades locked.

The single heartbeat where neither of us swung.

That moment is the reason I'm up here instead of downstairs.

That moment is the reason my hands won't stop shaking.

I release the railing and press my thumb into the center of my palm until the tremor quiets. My father trained me to hide every crack, every flinch, every stray emotion. Control is safety. Control is survival. Control is loyalty.

But in that split second—that impossible pause—control slipped.

She fought with the same precision I did.

The same restraint.

The same... purpose.

And she looked at me like she recognized something.

Something she shouldn't have been able to see.

Lightning fractures the sky, lighting up every mirrored surface across the tower district. The flash burns white against my vision—and then the thunder rolls in, low and uneven, like a warning.

Behind me, two palace sentries reposition. Boots scrape. Armor shifts. They're pretending they aren't watching, but they are. Surveillance doesn't sleep here. Dominion made sure of it.

A muscle in my jaw jumps.

I straighten my shoulders, smoothing my expression into the precise neutrality expected of me. I exist in this palace by never giving them anything to question. Anything to interpret.

But the storm presses closer, humming faintly against the railing. It feels like static crawling up my spine.

I lift my gaze into the rolling darkness.

Another flash—closer this time.

And in that blinding crack of light, something under my ribs jolts.

Like a pulse answering mine.

Like someone else is out there staring into this same storm, breathing this same charged air.

Like the sky itself is whispering:

I am not alone.

I swallow hard, refusing to name the thought.

Because I am alone.

I have to be.

But when lightning splits the sky again, something inside me answers anyway:

I am not alone.

And I don't know why.

✦ ☽⋆☾ ✦

Aly

The Undergrid never sleeps.

The whole district hums like a creature breathing—engines, power conduits, stray currents sparking through open seams in the walls. The air tastes like dust and electricity, sharp enough to sting my tongue.

I step out onto the balcony welded to our safehouse. The metal beneath my boots sags slightly, protesting with a groan. It's barely a balcony at all—just a slab of rust bolted to an unfinished frame of a collapsed tower.

But it's the only place I can breathe without eyes on me.

The wind whips at my braid, tugging strands loose. Moisture clings to the air, heavy enough that the next rain burst will be blinding. My ribs throb under the tight bandages. I inhale carefully, wincing as the pressure bites.

I should be inside, letting the healers finish.

I should be answering my mother's questions.

I should be pretending yesterday didn't get under my skin.

But I can't.

The arena is still there, replaying behind my eyelids every time I blink. The roar of the crowd dissolves first, fading like static. But the rest stays sharp—too sharp.

His blade catching mine.

The shift in his stance.

The moment neither of us struck.

I don't understand it.

I hate not understanding.

He could've killed me.

I could've killed him.

Both of us hesitated.

I grab the railing and lean forward, letting the city heat press up against me. Neon spills across my skin in fractured patches—blue on my cheekbone, violet across my throat, red against my palms.

I close my eyes, trying to slow my breathing. It comes uneven. Shaky.

He fought like someone who knew cages from the inside.

Someone who'd learned control the hard way.

Someone who wasn't a monster manufactured by the Empire, but a person shaped by pain.

And the way he looked at me...

Like I wasn't just another opponent.

Like he recognized something.

A low rumble shakes the scaffolding beneath me. I open my eyes to see storm clouds rolling over the high towers—thick, dark, brimming with silver fire. The wind shifts direction, cool for the first time tonight, brushing cold fingers across the back of my neck.

It feels like an exhale.

A warning.

A promise.

Lightning cracks through the sky, illuminating the towers so brightly the glass looks like it's melting. Thunder follows, rattling the balcony under my feet.

And then—just for a moment—something pierces through the ache in my chest.

A flicker.

A pull.

A quiet, impossible knowing.

Like someone far above is caught in the same storm.

Like their breath stutters at the same second mine does.

Like the world narrows to a single pulse shared across miles.

The words slip into my mind before I can stop them:

I am not alone.

I suck in a breath, startled by the thought. I straighten too fast, pain ripping down my side. The balcony groans, the Undergrid hums louder, and my mother's voice echoes faintly from inside the safehouse.

I shove the feeling down. Deep. Buried.

I reach for the door.

But the storm flashes white-hot, and something under my ribs stirs.

I am not alone.

The thought hits hard, unwanted. I hate that I don't know why—hate the certainty that someplace above me, someone else lifts their head at the exact same moment.

As if the storm is speaking to both of us.

As if we're not done with each other.

Not even close.

✦ ☽⋆☾ ✦

Lightning splits the sky one last time.

On the palace balcony, he lift his head.

On the rusted ledge, she does the same.

And across the miles of glass, neon, and silence, one truth echoes through the storm:

We are not alone.

Something in the storm makes sure they feel it.

Chapter 12: Years of Ash

Tiberius

Years don't move in lines.

They move in missions.

I don't feel them pass the way normal people do. There's no clean sense of *now I'm nineteen, now I'm twenty.* Just briefings. Extractions. Eliminations. The sharp click of a rifle lock, the white flare of a stun charge, the quiet after.

The quiet is always the worst part.

✦ ☽⋆☾ ✦

Year One...

"Again," Dominion says.

We're alone in the simulation chamber. No sentries. No advisors. Just us and the projection field humming in a low, hungry blue.

I stand in the center, weapon steady. Around me, rebels flicker into being—hard-light illusions coded from real faces. Some I recognize from dossiers. Some I've already killed.

"Priority target," Dominion says, voice mild. "Sector Twelve cell leader. Carmichael."

A woman's face resolves from static: sharp jaw, dark eyes, hair braided back and threaded with copper wire. She looks younger than the intel file. More alive.

Lara Carmichael.

Commander. Symbol. Problem.

"Your task?" Dominion prompts.

I lift the pistol. The projection's chest fluoresces with a softly pulsing mark: center mass.

"Neutralize," I say. My voice doesn't shake. It never does in here. "Efficiently. Cleanly. No collateral outside the declared target radius."

His mouth tilts. People call it a smile. They're wrong. "You're learning," he says. "But not yet."

He gestures, and the simulation shifts fast, too fast—allies popping in around Carmichael, blurred faces moving in front of her, taking hits that should've been hers.

"Empires fall," he says, "when you try to spare everyone." His gaze cuts to me. "This is why rebellions breed in the cracks. They believe their deaths *matter* more than the lives you protect."

I empty the clip. The false rebels shatter into light, one after another, until only Carmichael remains. She doesn't flinch. She looks right at me—a line of code wearing a human face—and lifts her chin like she knows exactly who I am.

The Ghost Prince.

The Tyrant's son.

I fire again. Her chest bursts into pixels. The sim goes dark.

"Better," Dominion says. "You're beginning to understand."

Am I?

The doors slide open. Advisors sweep in with their datapads and their hollow praise. I stand very still in the middle of the room, staring at where Carmichael's projection stood.

She was never really here.

I killed her anyway.

A ghost killing a ghost.

Time smears. I learn to move through it like smoke.

Sector raids at dawn. Quiet assassinations at dusk. Long hours in surveillance rooms listening to rebellions crackle across frequencies like static—so many voices convinced they're winning.

We let some strikes land.

We let some shipments go missing.

"We give them victories," Dominion explains one night, watching a glowing map of the colonies redraw itself in real time. "So they grow careless. Patterns reveal themselves when people believe they're safe."

I nod where I'm supposed to. I tell myself this is strategy, not cruelty.

But every time a red marker blinks on the map—*rebellion stronghold neutralized*—my chest tightens.

Did we let them live just long enough to find their names?

Did I?

I see their faces in my sleep.

Not for long.

Never for long.

Just enough to know I remember them.

✦ ☽⋆☾ ✦

Year Four...

I stand in a flooded alley on Kalos-3, rain pouring so hard the neon signs across the street bleed into rivers of color. My cloak is soaked. My boots are full of water. A body lies at my feet, half in shadow, half in the wrong kind of light.

He was my target.

He was armed.

He would've killed others.

None of that makes the alley feel less like a grave.

The comm in my ear crackles. "Status, soldier."

"Clean," I say. My voice sounds flat. Distant. "Target neutralized. No eyes."

For a moment, I don't move. I just stand there, letting the storm fall on my face, washing blood from my knuckles. Somewhere above the roiling clouds, the towers of Empyrium pierce the sky.

I tilt my head back, searching for a glimpse of home through the storm.

Home.

The word feels wrong. The city feels wrong. *I* feel wrong.

Lightning flashes, and in the stark white I see an arena floor. A girl's eyes fixed on mine. A moment where neither of us swung.

I'd almost convinced myself I imagined her. That the hesitation was weakness, nothing more, and I burned it out of my system like Dominion wanted.

And yet...

My fingers curl into a fist.

I am not alone.

The thought comes out of nowhere. Unwanted. It rattles me enough that I actually stagger a half step.

I exhale hard, forcing the air from my lungs, forcing the thought away. There is no one else. No one who knows what this feels like.

Just me. Just the work. Just the storm.

"Confirm exfil," my handler says through the comm.

"On my way," I answer, and turn my back on the body.

But the storm stays with me.

So does the feeling.

✦ ☽⋆☾ ✦

Year Seven...

By twenty-five, I am what they wanted.

Ghost Prince.

Executor.

Dominion's right hand.

The court whispers it like a title, like a curse. They don't know where I go when the palace lights dim. They don't know which orders come from Dominion and which ones pass through my hands first, filtered and altered in fractions small enough that no one notices but me.

No one's supposed to notice.

It's the only rebellion I can afford.

In the war room, holo-maps of the colonies hang in the air like ghosts of dead worlds. Rebel activity flares in red and amber, shifting as reports flood in.

Dominion stands at the center of it all—hands clasped behind his back, posture relaxed. A predator's stillness.

"Coalition cells are consolidating," an advisor says, indicating a cluster of symbols around the outer sectors. "Undergrid, fringe worlds, mining stations. They move faster now, but less carefully."

"Desperation masquerading as courage," Dominion murmurs. "They've tasted spectacle. They'll want more."

My gaze traces the highlighted routes. Supply runs. Extraction paths. Safehouse chains. There's a pattern forming—thin, faint, but there.

A name flares at one of the nexus points.

CARMICHAEL, LARA.

High-value target. Coalition Commander.

My spine goes rigid.

Dominion notices. Of course he does. His attention slides to me, sharp and assessing.

"Thoughts, Tiberius?" he asks.

I school my face into neutrality. "The cluster's overextended," I say. "If we hit here—" I gesture to a junction near the colonies' edge, "—we split their supply chain. Force Carmichael to expose more assets if she wants to maintain pressure along the inner sectors."

Dominion's lips curve, pleased. "Yes," he says. "But I want more than assets."

He steps closer to the projection of Carmichael's name and flicks his fingers. A hologram blossoms into the air—her face, older now than the simulation I saw seven years ago. More lines around her eyes. More weight in her shoulders. She looks tired.

She also looks... proud.

"Lara Carmichael fancies herself the people's blade," Dominion says. "Strike off the blade, the hand will flail. The body will bleed." His gaze slides to me again. "Unless the Ghost Prince prefers we let her play a little longer?"

The room chuckles politely. My stomach turns.

"What's the directive, sir?" I ask.

"Directive?" He considers the map, eyes half-lidded. "We set a stage. Feed them intelligence about a vulnerable convoy. Make sure Carmichael sees it as the opportunity she's been waiting for. Undergrid route, Sector Twelve. It has... poetry."

His smile doesn't reach his eyes.

"Then," he finishes, "we close the jaws."

The advisors nod, already inputting commands, crafting the bait, designing the illusion of weakness.

I stare at Carmichael's holographic face.

She looks like she knows it's coming.

She looks like she doesn't care.

She looks... familiar.

"Understood," I say, because that's what my position requires. "I'll oversee the operation."

Dominion's gaze sharpens, faint interest sparking there. "Will you now," he says softly. "Good. This is the kind of lesson that shapes empires, Tiberius. To rule, you must be willing to cut the rot from the bone. No matter how much it screams."

The map shifts again. Routes converge on Sector Twelve. The trap begins knitting itself together in light and data.

My chest feels too tight.

I tell myself it's because I'm calculating variables. Because I want to minimize collateral. Because if I'm there, I can aim the blade more precisely.

But under all of that, smothered and buried, another thought moves like a fault line.

What if we're the rot?

I blink the thought away before it can fully form. Before it can show on my face. Before Dominion can smell it.

The storm outside the palace windows rumbles, distant but approaching. I glance at the glass, at the city beyond, at the sky rolling dark over the towers.

Lightning flashes, turning my reflection into a stranger for half a heartbeat.

I hold my own gaze anyway.

I am not alone, the storm whispers, unwanted and impossible.

I shut it out.

I turn back to the map.

I start designing a trap I'm not sure I want to succeed.

Because this is what ghosts do in Empyrium.

We haunt the living.

We do as we're told.

And we try, in the smallest ways, not to become exactly what made us.

✦ ☽⋆☾ ✦

Aly

Seven years burn fast.

They don't feel like years. They feel like missions, like scars, like the split-second between the moment you step off a ledge and the moment you hit the ground—stretched out, repeated, normalized.

We call it resistance.

Sometimes it feels like drowning.

✦ ☽⋆☾ ✦

Year One...

The first year after the arena, my mother can still make me laugh.

On the days she wants to.

Tonight... she's somewhere in between.

We're hunched over a flickering holo-map in a cramped safehouse, Undergrid vent fans rattling above us like they're coughing on their last breath. The lights glitch again—cold blue, then too-bright white.

My mother swats the side of the projector with the heel of her hand. "If I die," she mutters, "it'll be because this relic blows a fuse and sets my hair on fire, not because some Empyrium dog gets a clean shot."

"That's inspiring," I say dryly.

She grins—sharp, quick, more teeth than warmth. "You want poetry or honesty, kid?"

I think about it.

Because with her, you always have to think.

"Both," I say.

She snorts, but there's the faintest spark of pride in her eyes—the kind she never names, never nurtures, just lets hover like smoke.

"Then you picked the wrong war," she says, "and the right side."

Her hair is coming loose from its braids. Without thinking, I reach forward and twist the closest strand back, weaving it into place with the familiarity of years. It's a gesture I've done since I was small, one she never asks for and never stops me from doing.

She goes still, just for a breath, letting me.

A rare softness.

A crack in the armor.

That's when she's most dangerous—when she lets me see the mother beneath the commander.

"You did good yesterday," she says, voice smoothing out. "Kept your people alive. You think I didn't catch that extraction route you improvised?"

I huff. "You also saw me almost get shot because the intel was bad."

Her hand finds the back of my neck—rough, warm, steady. "Almost," she says. "But not. There's a difference."

It feels like reassurance and reprimand rolled into one.

Classic Lara Carmichael.

I swallow. "We shouldn't have been there. It was a trap."

"Everything's a trap," she says calmly. "Ours. Theirs. Theirs disguised as ours. What matters is who walks out of it."

Her thumb rubs once at my neck, grounding me. Teaching me. Claiming me. Preparing me.

"You walk out," she says quietly. "You hear me? No matter what ash this empire turns us into, you walk out."

It hits something deep and aching—because she says it like she knows she won't.

Like she's already preparing me to stand where she stands.

To take her place.

To inherit her ghosts.

I wish I could promise her I'll survive.

I don't.

Instead I finish her braid the way she taught me years ago—firm, neat, unbreakable—and tuck the end into place.

"Storm's coming," I murmur, glancing at the window. Rain leaks through the cracks, smearing the city lights into blurred streaks.

My mother lifts her eyes to the sky like it's an old rival she's been outmaneuvering for decades. "Good," she says. "Covers our noise."

We lean over the map again, shoulders almost touching—not quite. Two shadows planning how to wound a monster without becoming one.

She shows me the routes, the choke points, the escape vectors.

She makes me correct her calculations just to see if I'll catch her mistakes—mistakes she places there on purpose.

She tests me. She trusts me. She pushes me.

Training me.

And pretending she isn't.

I don't know it then, but moments like this will gut me later.

Not on a battlefield—but in the quiet.

In the remembering.

Because she was not mine for long.

✦ ☽⋆☾ ✦

Year Three...

We're in a debrief and it smells like sweat, engine grease, and cheap coffee that's more bitterness than liquid.

The mission went "well" on paper.

We got the shipment.

We crippled an Empyrium supply line.

Only three civilians died in the crossfire.

Only.

General Tovren slams his hand down on the table, rattling empty cups. "They chose their side the moment they kept their heads down and let the Empire feed on them," he snarls. "Collateral is fuel. Bodies are symbols. The more the better."

I flinch.

Across the table, my mother's jaw goes granite-hard. "We don't kill to prove a point," she says. Her voice is quiet, but it slices through the room like a blade honed on truth. "We kill to prevent worse ones."

Tovren snorts. "You're getting soft, Lara."

"And you're getting reckless," she fires back. "You want to be a butcher, that's your business. But don't paint it in our colors and call it justice."

Several officers shift, suddenly fascinated with their datapads, caught between fear of her and the thrill of Tovren's brutality.

My chest feels like it's caught in a vise. The faces of the civilians blur behind my eyes—a woman shielding her child, a man dragging an injured stranger out of the blast zone.

Their screams don't care which side fired first.

"We can't win clean," Tovren says. "That's a fairy tale you tell your daughter so she can sleep."

The room goes very still.

My mother's gaze flicks to me—sharp, protective, dangerous—then back to him.

"My daughter doesn't sleep," she says. "She earns every hour she gets. And she's the reason we haven't crossed the line you keep sprinting toward."

Heat crawls up my neck. I want to disappear and stand taller at the same time. That's what she does to me—makes me feel both seen and overshadowed. Loved and crushed.

"Enough," one of the other commanders snaps. "We don't have the luxury for moral arguments. The Empire certainly doesn't."

"That's why we should," I say.

The words come out before I can stop them.

Every head turns.

My mother's eyes find mine.

There's a warning there, yes—but also something else:

Say it. If you're going to speak, say it fully.

"We're supposed to protect people," I say, voice raw. "If we start counting dead civilians as 'good optics,' then we're not better than what we're fighting. We're just... another kind of rot."

A silence drops over the table, heavy as ash.

Tovren sneers. "You're young," he says. "You'll learn."

Maybe I will.

Maybe I won't.

But I know this: every time we pick spectacle over protection, something in me pulls back. Refuses. Stays mine.

My mother sees it.

Tovren fears it.

After the meeting, my mother falls into step beside me in the corridor.

"That was dangerous," she murmurs. "Smart. But dangerous."

"You taught me to say the thing that needs saying," I remind her.

She huffs out something that might be a laugh. "Yeah, well. Sometimes I regret it. Doesn't mean I'd take it back."

I can't help it—irritation pricks under my skin. She raised me to speak my mind, but only on *her* timeline. Only when *she* approves the target. It's infuriating. It's caring. It's both.

We walk in silence for several paces. The lights flicker overhead.

"You were right," she says finally, so quietly I almost miss it. "Don't let them sand that edge off you."

"Even if it makes me a problem?" I ask.

She slings an arm around my shoulders, firm and warm and unbearably familiar. "Especially then."

I lean into her warmth for the length of three heartbeats.

I don't know it's a countdown.

I don't know I'm memorizing the shape of her arm around me.

I don't know how much of her I'll lose when she's gone.

But something deep inside me already knows:

This will be one of the last times she chooses mother over commander.

And it will break me when there are no more of them left.

Year Six...

Rain again.

It always seems to be raining when the world fractures a little more.

We're crouched on a rooftop two sectors from the palace line, the wind knifing sideways, rain soaking straight through my jacket. Below us, an Empyrium convoy crawls along a lower roadway like a trail of poisonous insects. My team waits in a tight formation behind me—one hand on the detonator, one hand on the rifle, eyes sharp, pulses steady.

They're waiting on *my* word.

My command.

My call.

Across the river of towers, Empyrium's high district glows like a nest of glass thorns—cold, perfect, untouchable.

I don't see him.

I don't hear him.

I don't even know if he's still alive.

I only saw his face once, half-hidden behind a mask.

But sometimes—especially in storms like this—I feel him.

A flicker under my ribs. A presence in the edges of my mind. A shadow threading itself through mine whenever lightning splits the sky.

I've tried to bury that moment in the arena beneath years of ash, missions, bad intel, worse choices.

It refuses to stay buried.

The way he moved.

The hesitation.

The question in his eyes.

The echo it left in me.

I breathe in the wet metal air and close my eyes for half a heartbeat.

I am not alone.

The thought hits as sharp as it did the first time—uninvited, unwanted, unchanged. My fingers tighten around the detonator.

"Commander?" Axel's voice crackles softly in my ear. Steady. Trusting. "We go on your mark."

My mark.

I open my eyes.

The convoy rolls into the kill zone—armored transport at the center, crates strapped down tight, weapons, tech we desperately need, maybe even something Dominion doesn't want anyone to see. We planned this strike for weeks. We modeled routes, blind spots, guard rotations. Everything hinges on this moment.

And then—

A child darts across the street below.

A small figure in a too-big coat, chasing something glowing and broken—a scavenged toy flickering with half-dead light. Their shoes splash in puddles. The guards don't notice. The world doesn't notice.

But I do.

My heart slams into my throat. "Hold," I snap.

The team freezes instantly.

I track the kid, every breath stretched thin. The toy skitters across the street. The child lunges after it. Thunder rolls so close it shakes water off the roof in sheets.

Come on. Come on. Come on—

The child reaches the far side, snatches the toy, and disappears into a narrow crack of alley.

Safe.

The moment they vanish, the street clears.

"Mark," I say.

Axel doesn't hesitate. My team doesn't question. They trust me even when I barely trust myself.

The explosions rip through the night—fire erupting in violent blossoms down the roadway. The convoy erupts into flame and smoke. Sirens wail in the distance. My team executes the extraction cleanly: fast, efficient, no unnecessary kills.

We vanish into the storm.

I tell myself the delay didn't matter.

Operationally, it didn't.

No one knows but me.

No one has to know.

But somewhere behind my ribs—under the bruises and the duty and the years of hardened ash—that small stubborn piece of me refuses, again, to die.

The piece my mother tries to protect.

The piece the rebellion keeps trying to stamp out.

The piece that feels a stranger's breath catch in the storm.

The piece that whispers back:

I am not alone.

✦ ☽⋆☾ ✦

Year Seven...

My mother's hair is streaked with more gray now, silver threads woven through dark. She wears them like medals instead of trying to hide them.

We're back over a map. Different safehouse. Different sector. Same storm grumbling outside the walls.

"Intel says the Empire's moving a high-value asset along an Undergrid route in Sector Twelve," General Tovren says, tapping a blinking point. "Light escort. No air cover. It's a gift."

"It's bait," I say immediately.

Heads turn.

Tovren sighs. "You think *everything* is bait."

"Because everything is," I snap. Then force myself to breathe. "Especially when it looks this easy."

My mother studies the map, brows drawn. She doesn't disagree. She never disagrees when it matters. That silence is worth more than anything Tovren spits out.

"We verify," she decides. "Cross-check signals, check for Ghost presence, watch patrol patterns for forty-eight hours. If it's real, we hit it. If it's not—"

"If it's not, we find out what they *want* us to do instead," I finish.

She nods once. A small, fierce spark of approval. Our minds braided together by too many campaigns to count.

Tovren scoffs. "While you two overthink it, the Empire will move the piece and we'll be left choking on the dust."

My mother's gaze sharpens like a blade being drawn. "You want to rush in blind, be my guest," she says. "But you don't drag my people with you."

I should be used to these arguments by now. I'm not.

Later, when the meeting breaks, I find her alone by the narrow window, watching rain streak down the cracked glass. Lightning flashes and makes her reflection look older than the woman beside me—older, but somehow more human.

"You're right," I tell her. "You know that, right?"

She doesn't look at me at first. Her eyes stay on the storm. "Some days," she whispers, "I'm not sure anymore."

The words hit wrong in my chest. "You can't say that," I whisper. "You're the one who keeps us from... from turning into them."

Her hand finds mine on the windowsill, fingers rough and warm. "Then you remember it for me," she says. "When I start to forget."

I blink hard. "That's not funny."

"I'm not joking."

She squeezes once. "Aly... you know what happens to people who do what I do, right? We don't retire to gardens and grandchildren. We burn hot and we burn out."

"Stop," I say. My throat tightens. "Don't talk like that."

She finally turns to face me fully, stormlight cutting across her features. "Listen to me." Her voice is steady—commander-steady, mother-hurting-steady. "There is going to be a day—soon or not—when you are standing in a room full of people who want to turn this rebellion into a hammer and smash everything just to hear the sound."

My eyes sting.

"On that day," she continues, "you will be the one who says no. Even if it costs you. Especially if it costs you. That will be your act of rebellion. Not against the Empire—against *us*."

"I can't do this without you," I say. I hate how small I sound. I hate that she hears it. I hate that she doesn't flinch.

Her smile is softer than I've seen in years. "You already are," she says. "You just don't see it yet."

Thunder rolls overhead, shaking dust from the ceiling. The storm presses closer.

She reaches up and tucks a loose strand of hair behind my ear—a gentle, mother-soft gesture that hits me so hard I almost flinch.

Then she steps closer. Drops her voice to a whisper only I can hear.

"Aly," she says, "if something ever happens to me—"

"Nothing's going to—"

"If," she repeats, sharper. "You go to the Data Vault. You find my file. All of it. Everything on me. You erase it. Every trace."

I freeze.

"Why?" My voice breaks around the word.

"Because the rebellion loves its martyrs, and worse still the empire will twist it the way they want it," she murmurs. "And I refuse to let them carve whatever story they want out of my bones. Promise me, Aly."

I shake my head. "No. No, I'm not—"

"Aly." Her hands come up and grip my shoulders. Firm. Anchoring. Loving in a way that hurts. "Promise me."

I swallow hard. "I—"

I can't say yes.

I can't say no.

I nod instead. Barely.

She accepts it like it's binding.

"Whatever happens in Sector Twelve," she says, "remember who you are. You're not my shadow. You're not their weapon. You are the girl who walked into an arena and refused to become what they wanted. Don't lose her."

I swallow, a raw sound tearing out of me. "You're coming with us," I say. "On this op. You know that, right?"

She hesitates.

It's tiny.

But it's there.

And it guts me in a way I don't understand yet.

Then she nods. "Of course," she lies.

I pretend I don't hear the lie.

Because if I acknowledge it, something inside me breaks early.

We stand in silence, watching the storm smear the city into shapes and shadows.

"I am not alone," I murmur without meaning to.

My mother tilts her head. "What?"

"Nothing," I say quickly. "Just—storms make me feel like... someone else is watching them too."

She gives me a look that's half amusement, half something like sorrow. "Maybe they are," she says softly. "We're not the only ghosts in this city, Aly."

She doesn't know how right she is.

And she won't live long enough to find out.

✦ ☽⋆☾ ✦

The night before Sector Twelve, the rain comes down hard enough to drown the streets.

On a palace balcony high above the city, a man I've only met once lifts his head toward the storm, guilt and duty and something nameless knotting under his ribs.

On a rusted ledge far below, I do the same, my mother's words and the weight of what's coming tangled up in my lungs.

Lightning splits the sky.

For a breath, the city disappears in white.

We are not alone, the storm whispers.

Something in both of us hears it.

Something in both of us believes it.

Even as our empires move us like pieces toward a trap that's going to break everything.

Part II

Inheritance of Ash

"Some inherit empires. Others inherit the damage empires leave behind."

Chapter 13: Broadcast of Fire

Lara

Sector Twelve smells like wet metal and trouble.

Lara knew the intel was wrong the second she stepped onto the catwalk.

Not because of anything visible.

Because nothing was.

Too still.

Too clean.

Too easy.

Aly stands to her right, posture precise, eyes sharp beneath the hood of her jacket. She doesn't use names in the field. Lara beat that instinct out of her before she could hold a blade or a gun.

"Commander?" Aly murmurs, barely a breath. "No movement. Nothing in thermal."

"That's the problem," Lara answers.

Aly's gaze flicks toward her—just a flicker, but enough. Lara sees the worry she tries to hide, the storm gathering behind her daughter's eyes.

Lara almost reaches for her.

Almost says *Go. Leave. Please.*

Almost breaks years of discipline.

But she doesn't.

She can't.

Not when Aly's life depends on Lara making the first move.

Thunder cracks overhead.

The quiet breaks.

A low hum shudders through the metal beneath their boots. Lara's eyes widen.

"Down," she snaps—

Too late.

A shockwave detonates under the catwalk—an EMP concussive blast that fries half their gear and sends soldiers sprawling. Drones explode from the shadows, rotors screaming. Ghost operatives drop down from the girders like falling blades.

Aly moves instantly, weapon drawn—

Lara seizes her wrist. Hard. "Not you."

Aly rips free, eyes flashing with fury—

not at Lara, but at losing her in the chaos.

"We hold the line," Aly spits, voice low, steady despite the storm inside her.

"No." Lara steps forward, putting herself between Aly and the advancing Ghosts. "You'll get out."

A stun round slams into the railing, showering them with sparks. Kai shouts for formation. Axel fires up suppression rounds. Their squad scrambles—

But the Ghosts aren't aiming at the team.

They are aiming at **Lara**.

Every helmet turns toward her with mechanical precision.

Aly sees it.

Her breath catches.

And something inside her breaks.

She surges forward—

not shouting a forbidden name, not breaking their cover—

but in a voice full of terror she never lets herself show:

"**Lara**..."

Her mother's name.

Not "Commander."

Not protocol.

Just **Lara.**

Said like a plea.

Said like a daughter.

Said like the world ending.

It hits Lara harder than the blast.

It is the closest she will ever hear to "Mom" in the field.

The only time Aly has ever said it in combat.

The last time she ever will.

Lara's heart fractures—and she uses the pain to move.

"Get her out!" she roars.

A Ghost blade slices her shoulder. Another catches her thigh. Lara barely reacts. She grabs Aly's vest, shoves her backward toward Kai with a commander's precision and a mother's desperation.

Aly lunges again—silent, deadly, fighting Kai with everything she has.

Axel curses, firing to cover them.

Aly's fingers claw the air, reaching—

Their hands brush.

Just once.

Just enough.

A spark of contact.

A lifetime in a single heartbeat.

Then Kai hauls Aly into the shadows. Aly twists, kicks, tries to break free—her face a silent scream, her hands still reaching for the mother she's losing.

Lara sees the moment Aly disappears from view.

Relief hits her like oxygen.

A Ghost baton slams into her spine.

Her vision whites out.

Her knees buckle.

The last thing she hears is Kai shouting for evacuation.

The last thing she feels is the ghost of Aly's hand against hers.

The last thing she thinks is the truth she can never say:

Stay alive. Please... stay alive.

Darkness takes her.

When Lara wakes, the world is small.

Steel walls.

Recycled air.

Lights dimmed to a bruise-colored dusk.

The kind of cell designed not to hurt the body, but to hollow out the soul.

Her mind swims, slow and heavy.

This is the third time she's surfaced like this—drugged, dragged back, dropped into the same metal box. Three days, maybe more, blurred by chemicals and interrogation lights.

Lara sits on the narrow bench, elbows on her knees, fingers laced so tight her knuckles ache. Her shoulders throb where the restraints dug in during transport. Her head is foggy from whatever drug they used to relocate her between sessions.

She remembers voices. Questions. The sting of cold restraints. Not answers—she never gave them that—but the rhythm of interrogation enough to mark the passing time.

Not hours.

Days.

She fights through the haze.

She forces herself to stay present.

She refuses to let the silence cannibalize her.

If she does, she loses the last thing she has left:

herself.

They've kept her sedated enough that consciousness comes in fragments—minutes, maybe an hour before they drag her under again.

Long enough to know she's not meant to survive this.

Long enough to realize the Empire doesn't need information from her.

They only need her death.

Lara stares at the small crack where the metal plates don't meet. Someone else etched a faint line there—years old, maybe decades.

She wonders if they survived.

She wonders if they broke.

She wonders if Aly is safe.

If Axel got her out.

If Kai kept her from coming back for Lara like the reckless, beautiful disaster she's always been.

The thought sends an ache through her chest sharper than any blade.

She closes her eyes.

Breathes once, steady.

If she dies here—and she will—that last moment with Aly will be the one that unravels her.

The stormlight in her daughter's eyes.

The tremor in her voice.

The whisper: *I am not alone.*

Lara had smiled at that, even through the battlefield noise.

Maybe you aren't, she'd wanted to say.

Maybe you never were.

But she didn't.

She couldn't.

Because the truth was too dangerous to speak.

A soft hiss breaks the stillness. The cell door slides open—only halfway. Just wide enough for a shadow to slip through.

The lights brighten slightly, recognizing an authorized presence.

A man in Executor black enters.

Lara's heartbeat stutters.

She knows that silhouette.

She knows that careful, quiet way he moves.

Leeon Holland.

He shouldn't be here.

He shouldn't look at her like that—with worry he is not allowed to feel, with grief he cannot afford, with something else beneath both that neither of them ever touched but always felt.

He keeps a precise distance.

Appropriate.

Unthreatening.

Being watched.

"Commander Carmichael," he says. The title is crisp, official, cutting.

"Executor Holland," she replies, matching his tone.

Both of them performing.

Both of them wounded by it.

"You're wasting your time," she says. "I've told your interrogators everything I plan to tell them."

"Which is nothing," he murmurs.

"Nothing," she agrees.

He steps half a pace closer—so small a movement the cameras might miss it.

"You've made enemies I cannot protect you from," he says quietly. "Not this time."

A truth wrapped in a lie.

A warning wrapped in heartbreak.

Lara swallows. "I know."

"You understand what that means."

You cannot save me.

She wants—god, she wants—to reach out.

To touch his wrist.

To lift her face toward his.

To say the words she kept buried for twenty-five years:

I should have told you about...

But she doesn't.

She can't.

If she reaches for him now, she destroys him.

So Lara straightens her spine.

Lifts her chin.

And gives him the only truth she can afford to speak aloud.

"The rebellion will not die with me."

Something passes through his eyes—fear? Confusion? The beginning of understanding?

He doesn't know she means *Aly*.

He won't know until it's far too late.

"You've made sure of that," he says.

She smiles—a small, resolute, devastating thing. "Yes."

He hesitates—one heartbeat of raw, unmasked pain—and then steps back.

The door slides shut.

The lights dim.

Lara exhales, shaky but quiet.

Her final thought is not fear—though fear coils inside her, human and trembling.

Her final thought is regret:

I should have said something...I should have told her.

Then darkness swallows her whole.

Tiberius • Age 25

The palace hallways gleam like they've been carved out of mirrors.

Everything reflects.

Everything repeats.

Even the sound of my father's boots echoes twice—once in the marble beneath him, once in my skull where years of conditioning have carved their own floors.

A squad of Ghosts marches behind us.

Grey walks at my left shoulder—close enough to read my breathing pattern, far enough not to draw Dominion's eye.

Between us walks the prisoner.

Lara Carmichael.

Her steps falter only once.

Not from pain—from defiance.

Dominion slows at the balcony doors and gestures without turning.

"Escort her."

My body reacts before my mind does.

I move to her side, grip her arm just tight enough to direct, not tight enough to bruise.

It's habit.

Instinct.

Training.

She doesn't look at me until the balcony doors hiss open and the storm-wind hits us both.

Then she turns her head.

Her eyes meet mine.

Something in her gaze flares—recognition, maybe.

Or grief so old it knows my face even if I've never seen hers before.

My breath stutters.

This shouldn't feel familiar.

Nothing about this should feel like déjà vu.

But it does.

She studies me for a heartbeat.

Then, very quietly—too quietly for the cameras, but loud enough for me—

"You look like her," she murmurs.

I blink. "Who?"

"Your mother," she says. "Not *him*."

The words slice into me like a blade.

Not because they hurt—

but because they *feel true*.

The air around me changes.

Not visibly.

Not audibly.

But inside my ribs—like something old and buried clawing its way upward.

She doesn't know what she just touched.

I was seven the last time I saw my mother.

Seven when Dominion told me she'd "died."

Seven when every file, every image, every piece of her vanished from the system in a single night.

He said she was weak.

Unfit.

A liability.

A lesson.

I learned it too well.

But there are pieces he couldn't erase.

Her voice.

Her scent.

The way she'd tie her hair back with a worn copper ribbon,

looping it gently around my fingers to make me laugh.

Lara's words hit that memory like a strike.

My mother.

Not him.

It shouldn't matter.

But it does.

I can barely breathe.

I want to ask—

I want to say something—

but her gaze shifts forward, and the moment is gone.

Behind me, Grey steps in closer—just half a stride—and murmurs, so quiet Dominion can't hear:

"Tiberius. You alright?"

I don't answer. My face stays carved from stone. But Grey's eyes catch the fracture anyway—a flicker, a breath I can't hide.

I don't tell Dominion what she said.

I never will.

The broadcast lights flare awake.

Dominion steps out onto the upper balcony, arms raised like an emperor of ghosts.

Lara stands in the center, wind whipping her hair, rain streaking her bruised cheek.

I stand to her right, two steps behind.

The place reserved for the weapon my father forged.

The Continuum amplifies Dominion's voice:

"Rejoice, citizens of the Empyrium—"

I tune him out.

I always do.

But I hear *her*.

Soft. Quiet.

For me alone.

"The rebellion will not die with me."

A flash of lightning illuminates her face.

She smiles.

Dominion doesn't hear it.

But I do.

A second later—

The blade falls.

Lara Carmichael collapses.

A scream tears through the crowd so raw it makes my vision jolt.

Not a cheering scream.

Not a protest.

A soul-breaking one.

I turn—instinct, not protocol—and scan the plaza below.

And I see her.

A hooded figure.

Far away.

Being dragged back by two others.

But she stops struggling for one heartbeat—just long enough to look up through rain and distance and chaos—and our eyes catch.

The girl from the arena.

Not a girl anymore—a woman.

Older.

Different.

Weathered by something sharp and brutal the last seven years carved into her.

Storm in her gaze.

Recognition in my chest.

Not a name.

Not a memory.

Just a pull—the same inexplicable pull I felt when our blades crossed in that arena.

My breath stutters.

She looks at me like she felt the same thing—

then she's gone, swallowed by the crowd and the storm.

I don't know who she is.

I don't know why seeing her feels like being struck by lightning.

I don't know why her presence feels like a warning and a plea at the same time.

I only know one thing:

I won't tell Dominion I saw her.

Not now.

Not ever.

She vanishes into the swarm of bodies.

And I do the only thing I can.

I look away.

Because if I don't, Dominion will see my face and know something cracked inside me.

I walk off the balcony, rain slicing across my uniform.

Grey follows silently, close enough to catch me if I fall apart—smart enough not to say a word.

For the first time in years, I feel something I cannot suppress.

Not guilt.

Not fear.

Humanity.

✦ ☽⋆☾ ✦

Aly · Age 25

I don't remember the tunnels.

Just the sound of my boots hitting metal steps, the sting of coolant vapors, the hum of distant generators. I claw my way out of the Undergrid like a ghost rising from a grave.

I shouldn't be here.

If Kai knew, he'd drag me back.

If Axel knew, he'd block the tunnel entrance.

If Vivian knew, she'd lock herself in front of the vent and scream until I couldn't make myself climb past her.

But I have to try.

I have to see her.

Even if it's hopeless.

Even if part of me already knows it.

I pull my hood farther over my head and round a corner, slipping into the shadow of a maintenance stairwell.

By the time I reach the lower freight platforms, the Continuum screens have already activated. Their light bleeds across the rain-slick towers like burning glass.

Crowds have already gathered—drawn like moths—to watch.

To *watch* their tyrant kill someone who spent her life trying to free **them** from *him*.

A sick wave rolls through my stomach.

I push past the bodies.

Harder.

Faster.

Like if I keep moving, the world can't collapse yet.

Then—

I see her.

My mother.

Kneeling.

Bound.

Bruised.

Alive.

Barely.

The world tilts under my feet.

The climb up to the Upper Spires happens in flashes:

Platforms.

Handrails.

Security lights slicing across my hood.

The storm swallowing the sound of my breath.

I reach the plaza just as Dominion steps onto the balcony.

And there—beside him—my chest caves in.

Tiberius Braxton.

Seven years since the arena.

Seven years since the storm felt like a heartbeat under my skin.

Seven years since that impossible, unbreakable moment—

And he looks almost exactly the same.

Tired.

Haunted.

Carrying too much for one body.

Not a monster.

Not the weapon his father claims he is.

Just a boy who grew into a cage.

Dominion's voice booms across the city:

"Rejoice, citizens," he says, voice booming across the square and through every Continuum broadcast. "For today, justice is delivered." I choke on air.

"No," I whisper. "No, no—please—"

"Commander Lara Carmichael," he continues, "traitor to the Empire, architect of sedition, murderer of hundreds—"

"Stop," I choke. "Stop lying—"

The crowd cheers.

Hollow.

Scripted.

Deafening.

They don't see her.

Not the way I do.

Not the way she kneels with her chin high, eyes burning, as if daring them to look away from their own cruelty.

Dominion lifts the blade.

"No—"

My legs buckle.

Kai and Axel aren't here—no one is—

and I take a step forward without thinking.

Another.

Another.

I'm five seconds from tearing straight through the line of drones hovering above the plaza when—

"Aly, stop!" Arms clamp around me from behind. Axel. His grip is iron, but his voice is breaking.

"You can't," he hisses. "He'll kill you—"

"I don't care—"

"Aly." Another voice, lower, steel-wrapped. Kai. He grabs my shoulders, turning me just enough to lock my gaze. "Look at me."

I shake my head violently. "That's my mother—"

"I know," he says, voice shaking despite the strength in it. "I know. But if you run, this ends with both of you dead."

On the screen, Dominion draws a blade.

A ceremonial one.

Elegant.

Curved.

Cruel.

My knees almost give out.

Kai holds me up. Axel holds my arm like he's anchoring me to life. Dominion lifts the blade.

"Lara Carmichael," he says, his voice suddenly soft—viciously gentle—"your rebellion ends today."

My mother lifts her chin. Her eyes burn with something fierce and proud and terrifying.

She opens her mouth—one last message, one last truth—but the Continuum cuts her audio.

The Empire doesn't want her to have a final word. The blade comes down.

My scream rips out of me like it's tearing through bone.

I scream.

I scream so hard my throat tears. Kai's hand clamps over my mouth.

Axel wraps his arms around me as my body collapses.

People cheer.

Screens flash red.

Propaganda banners unfurl like blood blooming across the sky. The weaponization of grief.

Public.

Efficient.

Total.

I don't feel my legs. I don't feel the ground. I don't feel anything but the hollow implosion in my chest—

Until I lift my eyes through the blur of tears—

And **he** is looking at me.

Tiberius.

Just for a second.

Just for a flicker in the storm of lights—

his gaze locks with mine.

Recognition.

Shock.

Pain.

Not just mine.

Then he turns away.

Sharply.

Like he didn't see me at all.

But I know he did.

And my heart doesn't break.

It freezes.

Hands grab me from behind—Kai and Axel, voices shaking, dragging me back before drones triangulate my position. I fight them.

I try to run back toward the balcony.

Toward my mother's body.

Toward the place where my world ended.

Kai pulls me into a run.

Axel shields my back.

The crowd swallows us whole.

Above us, the broadcast loops. Her death becomes an anthem.

And something inside me becomes a blade.

The rebellion will not die with her. She made damn sure of that.

She made me.
Aly Carmichael dies in that plaza.
Drowns in that scream.
Burns in that storm.
What rises in her place—
Alysa Tobias—
is something the Empire should have feared far sooner.

Chapter 14: The Ultimatum

Aly

The council chamber feels wrong.

Too large.

Too open.

Too bright for a room where they're about to decide who I'm allowed to be.

Three months since my mother died on a balcony carved from steel and cruelty.

Three months since I lost her.

Three months since my last anchor dissolved into rain.

I stand at the far end of the table, hood up, jaw locked, shoulders squared. Kai stands behind me—too close, too steady, too unreadable. Axel is near the door, arms crossed, foot tapping in a rhythm that only he hears. Vivian stands a step closer to me than she ever used to, tension in every line of her posture.

General Tovren is the first to strike.

"Three months without a leader," he says. "Three months without a face of resistance."

His gaze crawls over me like a weight.

"It's time," he says. "We need a commander."

General Aris Dane speaks next. His voice is smoke and iron.

"A rebellion without a spine collapses. The girl must step up."

Girl.

Not commander.

Not soldier.

Not anything I've bled to become.

General Cira Morn's eyes flick to me—quiet, assessing, almost protective. "She hasn't had time to grieve," she says. "None of us have."

"No one gets that luxury," Aris snaps. "Not anymore."

The pressure in the room tightens around my throat. My pulse hammers. I keep my expression still, steady, unreadable—exactly how my mother taught me. Her voice echoes under my ribs:

Don't let them see your fear, Aly. Fear is a weapon they will use better than you.

Tovren taps a datapad onto the table.

My name flashes across it.

Aly Carmichael—Restricted Lineage Clearance.

Like a blade tipped with poison.

"If you refuse leadership," he says, "your lineage becomes public. Dominion will hunt you the moment he puts the pieces together."

Axel takes a step forward, fury tightening his jaw. "You're threatening her."

"Protecting the rebellion," Aris counters.

Vivian shakes her head, voice sharp. "No. You're cornering the one person we can't afford to lose."

General Morn exhales. "Let her speak."

Kai moves just slightly, body angled toward mine. His voice is low, soft enough only I can hear.

"You don't have to take this," he murmurs. "We can restructure. Choose a council. There are other ways."

But I hear what he doesn't say—

If you refuse, they turn on each other. If you refuse, they fracture. If you refuse... she died for nothing.

Heat presses beneath my skin, sharp and rising.

They want me to inherit my mother's role.

Her war.

Her burden.

Her death.

Mother, I call her in my mind when I need to stay sharp.

Mom, only when the edges threaten to split.

Right now she is both.

And neither.

I lift my chin.

"If I lead," I say, "it will be on my conditions."

Silence slams through the chamber.

Tovren arches a brow. "Conditions?"

"My face stays hidden."

The murmurs are immediate, sharp, chaotic—

"A faceless commander?"

"We need a symbol—"

"She's being reckless—"

"She's being smart," Vivian snaps.

I continue before anyone can interrupt.

"No broadcasts. No portraits. No name tied to the rebellion. No public trace."

Morn studies me with interest. "You don't want power."

"I want protection," I say. "For all of us."

Tovren scoffs. "A leader without a face is no leader at all."

I hold his stare, voice steady as split steel.

"Then let them see a Ghost instead."

The room goes absolutely motionless.

Vivian whispers, goosebumps rising on her arms, "This is how legends start."

Kai's breathing changes—barely—but I catch it.

Aris Dane looks at me like he's evaluating a blade for flaws. "You would hide your identity from your own people?"

"To survive," I say. "And to make sure the rebellion survives with me."

Tovren leans back, expression thinning. "Very well. Ghost Commander."

The title hits me like a punch to the ribs.

Once, it belonged to my mother.

Now it becomes mine.

Not because I deserve it—

but because they've boxed me into a corner with no exit that doesn't end in blood.

Kai dismisses the room with a clipped, "Meeting adjourned."

The others file out—Tovren glowering, Dane unreadable, Morn offering me a single quiet nod that feels more like loyalty than anything verbal.

Only when the last door seals do I breathe.

Kai steps closer, gaze searching. "Aly—"

"Don't," I whisper.

He stops.

Vivian's voice softens. "You just took the weight of a war onto your shoulders."

Axel, voice rough, says, "And we're with you. Every step."

I nod, swallowing the pressure in my throat.

But inside—
my bones ache with the echo of a cage being built around me.
Somewhere in the empire, another child was shaped to fit a cage.
And now they want to build one for me.
I walk out of the chamber.
It doesn't feel like rising.
Or leading.
Or becoming anything worth applause.
It feels like burial.
And still—
I move forward.
Because I will not be shaped by any hand but my own again.

Chapter 15: Heir of Ash

Aly Tobias

I feel the cracking before I feel anything else.

A thin, hairline fracture running straight through my sternum.

Soft, invisible... but widening with every step I take.

Three months since my mother died in front of the entire Empire.

Three months since the scream tore out of my throat and left something in me raw and shaking.

Three months.

Not enough time to grieve.

Barely enough time to breathe.

And now I'm here.

In a chamber where the air feels too thick to swallow, where shadows cling to the walls like witnesses, where they want me to stand where my mother stood.

The ceremony is small.

Private.

Closed-circle only—the way my mother always intended leadership transitions to be.

Which is darkly ironic, considering she never wanted *this* for me.

My hood stays up.

My hands stay still.

My spine stays straight.

On the inside, nothing is straight.

Nothing is whole.

The room they chose is deep in the Undergrid, lit only by biolum strips and the flicker of a single failing lamp. Shadows crawl across the cracked concrete like ink veins. It smells like engine oil, old metal, and the faint sharpness of ozone from distant power conduits.

Fitting.

This rebellion was built in the dark.

Now they're asking me to stand at the center of it.

Kai stands near the center of the room, posture precise, mask-perfect, every inch the strategist my mother trusted with her life. Axel is near the door, jaw tight, eyes moving over the chamber like he's counting exits in case I bolt. Vivian is close—closer than anyone—hovering at my side like she's the only one who sees the cracks forming under my skin.

Tovren watches me with thinly veiled impatience.

Aris Dane watches me with cold calculation.

General Morn watches me with quiet concern.

They all expect something from me.

Something I don't know if I can give.

Kai lifts the dark strip of fabric—the Ash insignia.

My new chain.

"Alysa Tobias," he calls.

The name hits the air sharp enough to cut.

My chest tightens. Hearing that name—*the name I chose*—spoken aloud makes something in me shift. It feels like a cut and a shield at the same time.

No one has spoken that name out loud until now.

No one has dared.

It is my armor.

My shield.

The grave I buried Aly Carmichael in.

I step forward.

One step.

Two.

Three.

Measured.

Controlled.

Like my mother taught me.

I pretend they're steady.

They pretend not to see how tightly I'm holding myself together.

Kai's voice is steady. "This isn't a promotion. It's a burden. One your mother carried with honor. One you now inherit."

That word—inherit—makes something twist painfully inside me.

I bite my tongue hard enough to taste blood.

Kai ties the insignia around my arm.

Fabric against fabric.

Weight against skin.

It feels too heavy.

My mother wore this once.

I thought that memory would make me stronger.

It only makes it hurt.

"Alysa Tobias," he says, "you are now Ash Commander. You lead in the name of the rebellion. You command the Ash Cells. You are our Ghost."

Applause breaks around me—soft at first, then louder, echoing, filling the room with something warm I cannot feel.

Vivian moves before anyone else.

She steps into my space, hands on my shoulders, eyes searching my face beneath the hood.

"Aly," she says softly —*not* Commander, not Ash, not Ghost—"look at me."

I do.

Her eyes soften. "I know you feel like you're drowning."

The crack in my chest widens.

"But you're still here," she whispers. "Still breathing. Still choosing. And that matters."

I swallow hard. The motion hurts. "I don't feel strong."

Her thumb brushes my arm—the smallest touch, grounding.

"You aren't supposed to," she says. "You just have to stand."

Her voice wavers—the only sign she's been grieving too.

"I'm not leaving you," she adds. "Not now. Not ever."

A tremor runs through me. I hold still so no one else sees it.

Axel steps forward next, voice rough.

"I swear loyalty to you."

His eyes flick to mine.

"To *you*, Aly. Always. Not because you're her daughter. Not because they chose you. Because *I do*."

I nod—firm but not reciprocal.

He needs to see the boundary.

He does.

His eyes soften but he steps back without expecting anything more.

He means it.

He doesn't hide it.

I don't return it—not the way he wants—but I let my hand graze his forearm in acknowledgment.

He nods like it's enough.

Aris Dane is silent, assessing.

Tovren nods coldly, already imagining how to use me.

Morn gives a soft, steady bow that feels more genuine than anything else in the room.

Then Kai raises his hand.

"For the rebellion."

"For the rebellion," they echo.

Their voices resonate around me.

They fill the chamber.

They fill the air.

They even fill the cracks in the walls.

But not the cracks in me.

They cheer like they know me.

They don't know anything.

They're cheering for a ghost.

The insignia digs into my arm.

My throat thickens.

I can't breathe past the applause.

Vivian leans close, whispers, "It's okay not to be okay."

It nearly undoes me.

Kai dismisses the room.

The generals disappear into tunnels and shadows.

Axel squeezes my shoulder once before leaving.

Vivian lingers—waiting, watching—until I nod that I'll be fine.

Only then does she go.

The door shuts.

Silence rushes in.

Their voices still echo in the chamber, a pulse of unity, of conviction, of belief.

But it hits me wrong.

Too sharp.

Too hollow.

Maybe that's why it feels safer.
Because if they don't know me...
they can't lose me.
I bow my head.
Let the hood shadow my face.
This is who I am now.
A symbol.
A ghost.
A name spoken only in whispers.
Alysa Tobias.
The Ash Commander.
I should feel powerful.
Instead, as the echo of their voices fades, I feel—isolated.
Unseen.
Untouched by the warmth they project at me.
They don't know the girl who watched her mother die.
They don't know the fracture running through my ribs.
They don't know how close I am to breaking.
They only know the mask.
Alysa Tobias.
Ash Commander.
Ghost.
Lie.
Weapon.
I lower my head, the hood shadowing my face.
In the quiet, my pulse whispers the truth:
I wasn't ready for this.
But I'm all they have left.
And that, more than anything, is why I take the next step forward.

Chapter 16: The Empire's Ghost

Tiberius

The Zenith War Room looks like it was carved out of perfection.

White stone polished to a gleam.

Black glass floors that reflect every movement like a second version of yourself walking a half-step behind.

Screens suspended in rings like orbiting planets, each one flashing data streams, casualty maps, Continuum scans.

Cold.

Sterile.

Silent.

Just how Dominion likes his empire.

I stand at attention near the central table, hands clasped behind my back, eyes forward. I don't let them flick to the soldiers lining the walls or the Generals whispering over projections. I don't let them show irritation, disgust, fatigue—nothing but obedience.

Detachment is armor.

Detachment is oxygen.

Detachment is life.

Dominion strides into the chamber with the presence of a man who believes the world belongs beneath him. Conversations die mid breath.

"My Ghost," he says.

A title.

Not a name.

Never a name.

I bow my head. "Father."

He moves beside me, tapping commands into the hologram. Red ignition points flare across Undergrid sectors like spreading infection.

"Six months since Lara Carmichael's execution," Dominion says. "Six months since I cut the head off their pathetic insurgency."

My pulse stutters—a microscopic tremor in my palm.

I hide it instantly, fingers curling behind my back until the knuckles ache.

I hope he didn't see.

"Yet the rebellion grows," Dominion continues. "Like rot beneath a fresh coat of paint."

A General clears his throat from across the table.

"Sir, with respect—the insurgents reorganized faster than projected. They have a new commander—"

"A phantom," Dominion snaps. "This... *Ash Commander*."

He spits the title like poison.

On the map, red flares stretch wider.

Sharper.

More deliberate.

My jaw tightens. I force it still.

"They hide their identity," Dominion says. "No face. No biometrics. No surveillance imprint. A ghost leading ghosts."

A flicker scrapes the back of my mind.

A hooded figure in a storm.

A blade locking with mine.

The hesitation.

The feel of recognition like lightning in my ribs.

The girl from the arena, seven years older, staring at me with a look that shouldn't exist.

A forbidden memory.

Unwelcome.

Unasked for.

I crush it.

Bury it.

I cannot afford this.

Not here.

Someone else speaks. "Reports say this new leader makes split-second moral judgments—hesitates under fire, spares civilians, redirects assets—"

Dominion snarls. "Weakness."

But the word hits me differently.

Something sharp lodges under my ribs.

A tremor of disagreement.

A flicker of memory—a girl, refusing to kill even when the world demanded it.

I clamp down on it.

"Sir," another General says, "people are beginning to—"

"People are irrelevant," Dominion cuts in. "Fear will put them back in line."

He taps a final command.

The map bleeds red.

Then he turns fully to me.

"I'm sending you undercover."

My spine stays straight.

My face stays calm.

My pulse does not.

"To the Neon Markets first," he says. "Then deeper. I want to know who this new commander is. How they move. How they think. How to break them."

Break.

His favorite verb.

I lock my jaw. "Yes, Father."

"You will report everything," Dominion says. "Every whisper. Every rumor. Every face. Nothing escapes my notice through you."

I bow slightly. "Understood."

He studies me—that razor assessment he perfected on me since childhood, searching for weakness, hesitation, humanity.

I give him nothing.

"You did well with Carmichael's execution," Dominion says.

A muscle jumps in my forearm—the smallest, sharpest spasm.

I smother it so fast it burns.

"She smiled before she died," he adds bitterly. "As if she knew something I didn't. As if her death was a victory."

My breath catches.

Her last words echo again—the ones only I heard.

The rebellion does not die with me.

"She had nothing," Dominion scoffs. "She died for nothing."

No.

She didn't.

But I say none of it.

"I expect no further surprises," he says. "Find this faceless commander. Drag them into the light."

He dismisses me with a flick of his hand.

I turn to leave.

My reflection moves with me in the black glass floor—rigid, obedient, hollow. A weapon molded to a tyrant's liking.

But for one heartbeat, the reflection blurs—not the glass, not the light—**me**.

A crack in the mask.

A ghost looking back who doesn't feel like his.

I look away before it shows on my face.

"Go," Dominion says. "The empire moves through you."

"Yes," I reply.

A lie.

A fracture.

A whisper of something I'm not ready to name.

I walk out of the War Room with perfect posture, perfect discipline, perfect silence.

Inside, a tremor still runs beneath my skin—faint, controlled, unwanted.

And a memory I should've buried years ago stirs like lightning behind my ribs.

Something is breaking.

And for the first time,

I'm afraid it's not a weakness—but a warning.

Chapter 17: Smoke & Circuitry

Aly

The Nullborn District always breathes like a wounded animal—shallow, skittish, waiting for the next strike. The district always smells like burnt wires and desperation.

The tunnels below it are worse—warm metal, coolant vapor, sweat sinking into corrosion. The kind of air that sticks to your lungs for hours. I move at the front of our small unit, hood up, mask down, boots silent against the gridded floor.

Pipes hiss overhead, dripping coolant in thin silver lines. The walls sweat rust. The floor is a patchwork of metal plates salvaged from ships older than the Empire itself. Flickering lights cast shadows that stretch too long, bending around corners that shouldn't exist.

It's home to the people the Empire pretends do not exist.

The families we're here to pull out before the next sweep.

Vivian moves ahead of me, silent as a whisper. Axel covers our flank. Two Ash Cells split off into adjacent corridors, herding civilians in controlled lines—quiet, efficient, invisible.

We can't make noise here.

Noise gets kids killed.

A minute later, their leaders crackle through my comms—whispered confirmations that their assigned families are already in safe conduits. That leaves my unit as the last line, the shield behind everyone else

"Sector sweep in eleven minutes," Vivian murmurs through comms.

"Make it eight," I answer. "Empyrium patrol's could be ahead of schedule tonight."

We knew the Empire was speeding up its purges.

We didn't know they were this close.

Vivian's voice crackles softly in my earpiece. "Four Nullborn families secured. We are the last in the west corridor. But there's... movement. Ahead."

The kind that makes her voice tighten.

"Empyrium?" I whisper.

There is a pause.

"Not sure. But something else is with them."

Behind me:

Axel watches the shadows like he expects them to bite.

And he watches *me*, like any danger to the mission comes second to losing sight of my silhouette.

Seven months since my mother's execution.

Seven months since I dug myself out of that scream and put on a mask so the world wouldn't see what was left of me.

Seven months, and sometimes it still feels like I'm walking with cracked bones.

"Movement," Vivian murmurs in my earpiece, urgent and tense.

Her voice is strained barely a whisper in my ear. That's why I keep her close—she puts the mission above everything, even me. Even when she hates it.

I lift two fingers. We halt.

The displaced Nullborn families we're escorting—ten people, three children, one newborn wrapped in a repurposed jacket—all freeze behind us. Their breaths sound like they're afraid to be real.

I edge forward, scanning the branching corridor. A dim flicker of light pulses from a broken conduit above us, throwing shadows like knives.

Empyrium boots.

Close.

Too close.

"Patrol," I whisper. "Six, maybe eight."

Axel shifts beside me, jaw tight enough I can hear the grind of his teeth. "Tell me when to hit them."

"No hitting," I breathe. "Not today."

He bristles—not because he disagrees, but because he would burn himself alive before he'd let me take a risk alone.

Vivian inhales sharply. "Aly—"

"We're not fighting," I cut in. "We're getting them out."

Axel curses under his breath. "We don't have the numbers for a confrontation."

"We won't confront," I say.

This happens every time—someone wants to fight. Someone thinks violence is the only answer.

It isn't.

Not for me.

Not after watching what violence took from me.

"Silent evac," I order.

Our team shift immediately—hands pressing families deeper into the tunnels, ushering them down side passages, covering children's ears so they won't cry out.

Axel leans close. "You're sure?"

"No blood in these tunnels," I whisper. "Not tonight."

He nods.

Because he knows what I saw that day on the balcony.

Because he knows mercy is the only piece of my mother I have left.

Because mercy and survival are the same thing down here.

I motion our group into a narrow side conduit—barely a maintenance pipe—and press a hand to the smallest child's shoulder, steadying him as he slips through.

Boots strike metal somewhere ahead—steady, confident, then pausing.

They're hesitating.

Not all of them.

Just one.

The air changes—subtle, but sharp enough to feel in the bones.

The patrol rounds the corner.

Eight soldiers, rifles slung low, flashlights cutting through the dark. Close enough to touch.

One of them hesitates.

Not in fear.

In restraint.

A held breath.

A human pause.

The others don't notice it.

But I do.

A shiver crawls up my spine—a strange tug, like someone unclenching a fist inside my ribs.

Like mercy, swallowed back down.

Someone near the patrol hesitates.

I can't see who.

"Stay quiet," I whisper.

Our families press into the shadows. The newborn doesn't cry. Thank every god of the gutters for that.

The patrol passes.

Slow.

Deliberate.

Searching for something else.

Maybe for me.

My pulse thuds hard.

Boots retreat.

Lights fade.

Something inside me unwinds—slow, reluctant.

Axel leans in. "That was too close."

"Close is better than dead," I say.

When the last echo disappears, Vivian emerges from the shadows ahead us, her shoulders dropping with relief.

"You could've given the signal to take them," she whispers. "We had angles."

I shake my head. "No one dies tonight."

Axel gives Vivian look that says, *don't push it.*

She doesn't.

We led the last of the civilians toward the safe conduit that will take them to the Undergrid holding zones.

A child clings to my sleeve as we walk—a small girl with oil-smudged cheeks and bright silver eyes.

"Are the bad men gone?" she whispers.

I swallow the sting in my chest.

"Yes," I say softly. "They're gone."

She nods, trusting me completely.

If she knew how close they were...

How one wrong sound could've ended all of us...

How someone among those soldiers hesitated in a way that felt like recognition...

She squeezes my hand tighter.

"Thank you," she whispers.

For a moment, something warm breaks through the cold armor in my ribs.

We slip deeper through the conduit. Pipes groan overhead, rattling coolant in broken rhythms. The lights flicker out entirely for a second, plunging us into perfect darkness.

It feels familiar.

The kind of dark I grew up in.

The kind of dark I learned to breathe through.

As we walk deeper into the tunnels, I can't shake the feeling that something—someone—was watching me.

Not hunting.

Not hostile.

Just...

close.

Too close.

A presence my mind can't name yet, but my bones recognize anyway.

A phantom in the dark.

A ghost in the empire.

And for a split second, I swear the air tastes like stormlight.

"Evac point ahead," Axel murmurs, voice low enough only I hear. "Thirty meters."

He touches my back—quick, grounding—a soldier's guidance, but the warmth behind it burns a little too honest.

I don't respond.

Not with words.

Not with anything that would confuse him more than he already is.

We emerge into a wide junction chamber filled with old machinery. The exit vent is half-collapsed, but still usable.

"Move," I signal.

One by one, the families climb through.

Vivian goes first, scanning every angle even as she moves.

Axel waits beside me.

"You good?" he whispers.

"Yes."

It's a lie.

He knows it.

"Still here," he murmurs. "Still with you."

I look at him in the dim light.

I don't say thank you.

I can't.

Not when gratitude might sound too much like something else.

When the last of our evacuees slip through, Vivian signals from the other side.

"All clear."

"Go," I tell Axel.

He hesitates—only for me—then disappears through the vent.

I take one last look down the tunnel.

The patrol is gone.

But the air still hums like someone was just here.

Like someone saw me—or almost did.

A cold pulse tightens behind my ribs.

Whoever hesitated back there...

They weren't a civilian.

And they weren't one of mine.

I slip into the exit vent and seal the grate behind me.

Time to vanish.

Tiberius

The tunnel air tastes like metal and static.

My unit checks the junction ahead, rifles up, visors down, every breath controlled.

Grey brings up the rear, silent as shadow, eyes tracking every angle I don't.

I hang back a few steps, scanning the walls, the floor, the air itself.

We just missed someone.

I can feel it.

A canister still warm against the wall.

A footprint half-smudged.

The faint impression of bodies pressed into shadow.

Efficient.

Quiet.

Precise.

Not Carmichael's old methods.

Someone new.

"Sector clear," one of my soldiers calls.

It isn't.

The quiet here feels... shaped.

Like someone held their breath until the patrol passed.

Like mercy pressed into muscle memory.

A strange, electric pull crawls up my spine.

Someone was here.

Someone close.

Close enough I should've heard them.

Close enough I should've *known* them.

My scanner blips once—faint thermal residue, fading too fast.

My chest tightens.

"The Ash Commander," I murmur without meaning to.

Grey glances over, sharp, the only one close enough to hear the words leave my mouth.

"Say again?" he murmurs.

I shake my head once—clipped, final.

"Nothing."

Grey doesn't push, but his eyes stay on me a moment too long.

He felt the shift in me. He always does.

I step deeper into the tunnel.

The air hums—warm in a way it shouldn't be.

Like a presence just slipped away.

Like a ghost moving out of reach.

"Move out," I order.

My soldiers march.

Grey falls in beside me, voice barely above breath.

"You felt something."

His tone isn't accusation. It's observation.

I don't answer. I don't trust what might come out if I do.

I linger a heartbeat longer.

Whoever I nearly found...

whoever hesitated in that moment of restraint...

They're not like the others.
And I can't shake the feeling I've crossed paths with them before.
A familiar echo.
A storm under the skin.
I exhale, steady.
"Next time," I murmur.
Grey hears that too—and this time, he doesn't pretend he didn't.
Next time, I tell myself.
Next time, I won't be a second too late.

Chapter 18: The Braxton Line

Tiberius

Dominion's private study is the opposite of the War Room. It smells like old paper and cold metal—a contrast to the polished perfection of the Zenith levels. Shelves line every wall, filled with relics of empires he's crushed, books he never read, and bottles of wine he opens only for theatrics.

The War Room is a machine.

This place is a shrine.

Gold-veined stone walls, obsidian shelves lined with relics from fallen nations, a single glass decanter of deep red wine pulsing softly with Continuum tags. A room designed to make anyone inside feel small.

Except me.

I'm not supposed to feel anything.

I stand where Dominion expects: centered, still, composed. A silhouette of obedience.

He pours himself a glass without offering one to me. He never does.

The wine glows faintly when he lifts it—data-threaded, laced with encrypted neural access. He sips like it's blood.

"We are approaching a new era," he says.

His voice fills the room the way smoke fills lungs.

"The Continuum has proven capable of stabilizing civilian compliance. But imagine..." He turns toward the city through the wall of glass. "Imagine if the chain of command could be digitized. No hesitation. No emotion. No weakness."

My spine stays straight.

Inside, something coils.

He continues, "Human decision-making is flawed. Delay, doubt, disobedience—these things cost empires." He glances at me over the rim of his glass. "But if we embed directive protocols into the officer network... decisions will trend toward perfection."

Perfection.

Meaning control.

Absolute.

Unbroken.

Unquestioned.

I keep my voice even. "At what level would this begin?"

"At the top." He smiles. "With you."

A pulse of cold runs through me.

Not the surface kind—the deep kind.

The kind that sinks into the bone.

To digitize command...

would mean digitizing me.

My thoughts.

My choices.

My hesitations—erased.

My instincts—overwritten.

My humanity—replaced.

A version of me without even the cracks.

A ghost wearing my skin.

For one breath, horror flickers so sharply I feel it in my teeth.

Then I bury it before it can reach my face.

Before Dominion can see it.

Because if he sees it?

He'll dig.

And if he digs...

Grey flashes through my mind.

Grey, who always stands behind me in silence but sees more than he should.

Grey, whose loyalty is real—not programmed.

Grey, who Dominion would reduce to circuitry without hesitation.

A soldier with no will.

No self.

No choice.

No one should have their will stripped from them.

Not even him.

I crush the thought before it shines through my expression.

"And then," Dominion adds, "through every commander. Every officer. Every soldier. The Continuum will become the Empire's new spine. And I will be its mind."

He turns back to the desk, swiping through encrypted documents, plans, projections—all threaded with red markers.

I recognize some sectors.

Undergrid.

Nullborn territories.

Ash cell routes.

"You expected the rebellion to collapse after Lara Carmichael," I say.

Dominion stills.

Slowly turns his head toward me.

A thin, razor-edged pause stretches between us—the kind that measures loyalty, not conversation.

"...Bold observation," he says at last.

Not praise.

Not anger.

Just testing.

Weighing.

I don't shift.

I don't blink.

I let the silence shape itself into obedience.

Only then does Dominion continue, as if I never spoke at all.

Then nods. "Of course I did. Her death was a spectacle. A warning. A clean end."

The image flashes without warning:

Lara kneeling.

Her chin lifted.

Her eyes steady.

Her last words—the ones only I heard.

The rebellion does not die with me.

I force the memory back into its cage.

Dominion snarls, "But instead I get... this. A ghost wearing Lara Carmichael's legacy like armor."

A projection flares to life on the desk—the Ash Commander's symbol.

No face.

No identity.

No trace.

"I want to know who they are," Dominion says. "Your undercover work should have produced results by now."

"It's not that simple," I reply.

His gaze sharpens. "Complexity is an excuse. Not an explanation."

I drop my eyes in practiced obedience.

Inside, nothing bows.

He continues pacing.

"This new leader moves differently. No patterns. No trail. No fear. They are deliberate. Surgical. Almost—"

his voice sharpens with smug satisfaction,

"*—almost the way I trained you*. The same precision. The same instincts. A shadow cut from the same mold. Only they lack the discipline. "

The words hit harder than they should.

A crack of lightning behind my ribs.

For a split second—just a breath—

the War Room dissolves into the memory I've tried to cauterize for years.

A ring of metal.

The roar of a crowd I couldn't hear through the helmet.

A blade flashing in dim light.

A girl's eyes—

indigo, furious, trembling, alive—

locked on mine.

And the hesitation.

Hers.

Mine.

That impossible, shared pause no training could explain.

My pulse stutters.

I shove the memory down so violently my throat aches.

It doesn't disappear.

It lingers.

Hot.

Bright.

Dangerous.

Dominion doesn't notice.

Of course he doesn't.

He thinks hesitation is a flaw he beat out of me years ago.

He doesn't see the cracks.

He never thinks to look.

Because I don't give him a reason to.

He taps the datapad again. "Almost exactly like you. Interesting, isn't it?"

I school my expression into perfect stillness.

"Coincidence," I say.

A lie heavy enough to bow bone.

Dominion hums, unconvinced but uninterested. "Whoever this 'Ash Commander' is... they think like a ghost. *My* ghost."

I should say something.

I should tell him the truth pulsing under my sternum—

that something in me recognizes this commander in a way I can't explain.

That the hesitation in that tunnel felt like looking into a mirror in the dark.

But another truth burns hotter:

If I tell him what I suspect,

he'll hunt her with everything he has.

And I—

I don't know why

but I can't let that happen.

"Find them, my Ghost," he says turning back to the datapad

So I bow my head.

"Understood, Father."

A lie.

A fracture.

A warning in my own voice I pray he doesn't hear.

There is someone out there who inherits Lara Carmichael's fire.

Dominion thinks it's a threat.

I think it's a promise.

I keep the thought buried.

Dominion taps the projection and it pulses, alive with surveillance logs.

"Find them," he says. "I don't care what it takes. Tear apart every shadow in the Undergrid. Drag this leader into the light."

A beat of silence hangs in the charged air.

"Yes, Father," I say.

He watches me—that brutal, precise gaze that once measured my worth like a blade on a scale.

I give him nothing.

No doubt.

No fear.

No flicker of the truth.

"Good." He dismisses me with a flick of his hand. "Do not return with failure."

I turn toward the door.

My reflection moves in the black glass.

Controlled.

Perfect.

Hollow.

A weapon carved from someone else's ideals.

But as I step into the hall, something in my chest stays hot—a flicker of lightning trapped under bone.

A warning.

A beginning.

A fracture in the line I was born into.

And I don't know what terrifies me more—

That I'm starting to feel it.

Or that I'm starting to want it.

Chapter 19: Counsel of Ashes

Aly

The strategy chamber hums like a live wire. Screens flicker with red-lined districts, casualty projections, comm interference maps—data laid out like a confession. The air smells like dust and recycled heat, like a room that hasn't slept in days.

No one is sitting.

Kai stands at the head of the table, arms folded, jaw carved from stone. Vivian circles the display like she's hunting it.

I lean on the edge of the table, keeping my breathing even. I haven't stopped shaking since the raid, but no one needs to see that. Commanders don't shake. Leaders don't get rattled. That's what everyone expects—what I was raised to perform. The problem is I don't *feel* like a commander. I feel like someone wearing the title like a borrowed coat, too heavy in the shoulders.

Kai clears his throat. "We need to slow down."

Vivian snaps her head toward him. "Slow down? We lost two safehouses last night. We're bleeding out."

"And charging blind will get us buried faster," Kai says, voice soft but sharp. "Dominion's countermeasures aren't improvised. Someone's feeding him intel. We stop the leak first."

Vivian laughs—short, humorless. "Of course. Patience. Your favorite disguise for inaction."

Kai doesn't rise to it. He never does. His restraint makes her fury look louder.

He looks at me instead. "Aly. You've seen Dominion's tactics firsthand. You know he's steering the narrative. If we make a move now without understanding the pattern—"

"We'll be reacting, not leading," I finish.

Vivian shoots me a betrayed look. I try not to flinch under it.

Leadership feels like this sometimes—choosing between two people you respect and knowing you'll lose one of them in the process. I've been in firefights with easier odds than this room.

"You're siding with him?" she accuses.

I swallow hard. My pulse stutters. Kai holds my gaze, steady, waiting—not pushing, just offering clarity in the noise. But even that feels like a weight I haven't earned. People look at me like I know what I'm doing. Like I know how to win wars, how to outmaneuver empires.

The truth is simple and ugly:

We can't win a street that already belongs to someone else's story.

My mother used to tell me that strategy isn't about bravado—it's about who *owns the frame*. Who controls the air the story breathes in. I didn't understand it then. I do now, painfully.

I straighten. "We don't need louder moves. We need quieter ones."

Vivian's eyes narrow, and guilt curls low in my stomach. She thinks I'm abandoning her. Maybe I am. Maybe being a leader means choosing the colder path and learning to live with the frostbite.

Kai tilts his head slightly—approval without victory. He never gloats. It's one of the reasons I trust him.

I continue, slower, choosing the words that feel like they were carved into me during the war for my own survival, words that echo in my mind from years of my mother sharpening it into something that is only mine:

"You don't win by shouting over your enemy," I say. "You win by taking away the room where their voice echoes."

The chamber goes still.

Kai breathes out—something between relief and recognition. Vivian looks like I slapped her with silence itself.

Part of me wants to take the words back, soften them. But leaders don't get to soften things. They get to be obeyed or blamed. Sometimes both.

I push off the table. "We choke the leak. Seal the channels. Control the narrative before it controls us. Win the silence... before we win the street."

The room shifts. Just slightly. But enough.

Kai nods once, decisive. "Then that's our next move."

Vivian storms out. She'll cool down—or she won't. But the path is set.

The weight of the choice settles in my bones, heavy and metallic. Every commander I've ever admired would say this is the moment leadership becomes real—not in the victories, but in the fractures. In the people who walk out of the room because of you.

I'm not sure I like it.

Strategy over impulse.

Silence over fire.

A move my mother would understand—maybe even approve of.

But it doesn't feel like approval. It feels like responsibility compressing around my ribs.

Still... this choice is mine.

And as the quiet expands through the chamber, I feel the world start to pivot on it.

Chapter 20: The Ghost Market

Tiberius

The Neon Markets always feel like they're breathing.

Not with life—with pressure.

Like the whole place is exhaling steam and neon light just to keep itself from collapsing in on the weight of everything unsaid.

Blue signs flicker overhead, throwing fractured light across wet pavement. Vents along the walls cough out heat in irregular bursts. The air tastes like metal and salt and cheap synth-spice, the kind that coats the back of your tongue and makes you want to swallow twice.

I pull my hood lower.

Blending is easy when you know what predators look like—and how to pretend you're not one.

The crowds press shoulder to shoulder, shifting in waves as hawkers shout their deals:

"Five creds for fresh greens!"

"Two for protein squares—no questions asked!"

"Skinners out tonight—keep your tags hidden!"

Noise, color, human desperation. A perfect labyrinth for smuggler routes. A perfect hiding place for rebellion messengers. A perfect hunting ground if you know how to listen.

I weave through the masses, scanning faces, tracking patterns.

Runners exchange coded taps.

Vendors glance twice at certain customers.

Narrow doors open for exactly three seconds—no more, no less.

All signs of supply lines.

All signs of the rebellion.

All signs of whoever the hell this *ash commander* is—the one person whose movements I can't get a single clean trace on. Dominion wants them ghosted. I want to understand them.

I'm not sure why.

I turn down a narrower lane, less lit, half-shadowed. A patrol booth hums at the far end—sensors scanning wrist tags, movement patterns, stress signatures.

Grey's voice crackles softly in my ear.

"Status?"

"Routine sweep," I murmur.

"You sound... off."

His tone is careful—quiet concern hidden under protocol.

"I'm fine."

Grey doesn't believe me, but he knows better than to press with open comms.

That's when I see her.

A small Nullborn girl, maybe eight. Too thin, clothes too big, wrist glowing faintly with the pale scar of the brand assigned to children born without recorded lineage.

Unprotected. Unwanted.

Easy prey for a patrol.

She reaches toward a fruit stall with trembling fingers. Bruised fruit. The kind no one would miss.

Except the vendor sees.

His hand lifts—not to stop her softly, but to strike. To make a lesson of her.

Grey whispers sharply in my ear:

"Sir—don't intervene. Booth sensors might—"

Before I can think, before I can calculate the consequences, my feet move.

Not close enough to draw attention. Just close enough to let the vendor see the expression beneath my hood. I let him catch one glimpse—one *second*—of the part of me Dominion forged.

Cold.

Controlled.

Lethal.

The vendor freezes mid-swing.

The girl bolts, vanishing into the crowd like smoke.

I don't report her.

I should.

Every part of my training screams at me to flag the incident, to mark her for relocation, to keep order clean and unbroken.

Instead I stand there, staring at the spot where she disappeared, feeling something rupture deep inside—quiet but unmistakable.

The first true act of rebellion isn't loud.

It's a whisper that doesn't go away.

"Tiberius," Grey murmurs, "you okay?"

No one should have their will stripped from them.

Not a child.

Not a soldier.

Not even Grey.

"I'm fine," I say again, steadier.

I'm not.

The rupture inside is small but real.

I turn—

And freeze.

A hand.

Just a hand at first. Pale, slender, steady. Reaching for the same bruised fruit, not stealing, not hiding—simply choosing. Her movement is practiced, economical, but there is something about the way her wrist turns, the surety of the gesture, that hits a pressure point in my memory.

The arena.

The girl with fire behind her eyes and mercy in her hands.

No.

This woman moves differently—quieter, contained, blending instead of blazing. But something in the shape of her silhouette snags at me like a hook.

She picks up a few pieces of fruit. She analyses each one, not with greed—with familiarity.

Survival familiarity.

Then I see the Nullborn girl again—the same child I saved—hovering near the stall, as if unsure whether she's allowed to exist here.

The woman with the fruit turns to her. No hesitation. No calculation.

Just calm, instinctive compassion.

She shifts half her basket into the girl's hands.

Not a performance. Not pity.

A choice.

My breath stutters.

Grey's voice softens in my ear.

"Sir? You stopped walking."

I don't answer.

Her hood hides her face, but mercy has a shape. A rhythm. A gravity.

And I've only ever seen that gravity once.

In the arena.

In her.

My pulse fractures into too many pieces to gather.

This is impossible.

Or—

No.

It's not impossible.

It's *obvious.*

Painfully, dangerously obvious.

My mind makes the connection in a single, silent snap.

The exact kind of pattern Dominion trained me to see.

Mercy under pressure.

Instinctive protection of the weak.

Precision in movement.

Stillness before action.

Fire buried under control.

All the traits he told me to hunt.

All the traits he said belonged to the Ash Commander.

All the traits I saw once before, in a metal ring, under dim lights, staring back at me through the eyes of a girl who should have hated me.

I feel the truth crystallize.

Clear.

Undeniable.

If I let myself take one more mental step, if I even *think* the words—

She is the Ash Commander.

—Dominion will feel it the moment he looks at me.

He always does.

He carved obedience into my bones; he knows how my mind moves.

He would sense the shift.

He would dig until he finds her.

And I—

I'm not ready to hand her over.

Not to him.
Not to anyone.
So I force myself back from the brink.
I don't deny the truth.
I don't question it.
I just don't let it fully form.
Restraint.
Controlled silence.
My own small act of rebellion.
Because I want to know for myself who she is.
Not the mask.
Not the symbol.
Her.

I catch myself leaning forward—just slightly—as if drawn to her by a tether I'm only now admitting is there.

Danger.
Not to her.
To me.
Grey again—quiet, confused:
"Sir? You're sure you're fine?"
I force breath back into my lungs.
"I said I'm fine."
I tear myself away.
Turn down the next alley.
Push the world back into its ordered shape.
But the crack inside me doesn't seal.
It widens.
Grey's voice fades into static as I move out of range.
And the truth I refused to name lodges under my ribs, hot and pulsing:
I know exactly who she is.
And I'm choosing not to say it.
Not to him.
Not yet.
And deep in that widening space, something dangerous begins to take root.

✦ ☽ ⋆ ☾ ✦

Aly

Neon always makes everything look softer than it is.

Warm blues and violets spill across the street like spilled ink, hiding the sharp edges of the market beneath a curtain of color. It's a trick—beautiful, effective, deadly. You drop your guard under lights like these.

I keep mine firmly in place.

Hood down.

Shoulders relaxed.

Movements fluid.

Invisibility is not just survival—it's strategy. People don't fear shadows. They forget them.

But the truth is, I'm tired of being forgotten.

The rebellion sees the Ash Commander.

The symbol.

The weapon.

No one sees me.

Except—

I slip through the vendors' calls, letting them wash over me:

"Fresh spices! Trade or coin!"

"Need a clean ID? Two-minute prints!"

"No Empyrium patrols this way—good prices tonight!"

The market is loud.

Alive.

But beneath the noise, there's a rhythm you can feel if you've lived in it long enough: coded knocks behind metal shutters, timed exchanges of small packages, glances that last exactly one heartbeat.

These are the lanes I walk.

The shadow currents.

I stop at a fruit stall, fingers brushing the produce. Soft skin, bruised edges, uneven shapes—the rejects from upper districts. People down here don't care. Food is food.

I'm calculating how much I can carry when something shifts behind me.

A presence.

Not threatening.

Not cold.

Just... aware.

Warm, somehow.

Focused.

Sharp in a way that makes my heart thud once, too hard.

It feels like being recognized by a memory I don't have.

A strange, fragile thought flickers:

Did they find me? Did someone finally see past the hood and mask and titles?

But no—

This doesn't feel like threat.

It feels like **attention.**

Like someone watching me the way people watch stars they're afraid to touch.

I don't turn.

Turning is how you give yourself away.

My mother drilled that into me: *Always feel first. Look second. Move last.*

I breathe out slowly, forcing my attention back to the fruit.

A small hand bumps my elbow.

A Nullborn girl looks up at me, eyes wide, hollowed by hunger and too many nights without a safe place to sleep.

I don't think.

I don't weigh the risks.

I just act.

I shift half my basket into hers. Bread. Fruit. Nuts. Enough for a few meals.

She blinks like she's not used to kindness.

Maybe she isn't.

Something in my chest tightens—the part of me my mother warned me would always be both my weapon and my weakness.

Mercy is a blade too, Aly. It cuts the world open differently.

What she didn't tell me was how much it would carve out of *me*, too.

The girl disappears into the crowd, small shoulders straighter than before.

The presence behind me pulses again—closer this time.

A breath not taken.

A sound not made.

A warmth like standing too near a forge.

My heart jumps.

Not in fear.

In recognition.

My fingers grip the edge of my basket.

Why does this feel familiar?

I turn, fast—

And see no one.

Only the press of bodies and the waterfall of neon light.

Only strangers.

Only shadows.

But the echo remains in my ribs, pulling like a string knotted to something I've never touched.

Something I feel like I *should* know, like a name on the tip of my tongue that refuses to form.

I swallow hard and scan the crowd one more time, slower, softer.

Nothing.

Still... I can't shake the sense that someone saw me.

Not saw *through* me.

Saw *me*.

Not the commander.

Not the ghost.

Not the legacy I inherited from my mother.

Just the girl she raised in silence and fire.

For a moment, I almost step after that feeling—that presence—just to see where it leads.

But reality presses back in:

Supplies.

Routes.

The outpost is waiting.

People are counting on me.

And maybe that's the cruelest part—the way leadership demands you walk away from things you're not allowed to want.

I disappear into the neon current.

But the warmth stays lodged under my skin like an ember that refuses to go out.

And somewhere deep in my chest, something I can't name...

stirs.

Chapter 21: The Weight of Silence

Aly

Rain crawls down the pipes in thin, metallic threads.

Not real rain—the Undergrid never gets real rain—just condensation from the upper tiers bleeding through cracked vents and rusted seams. It drips in irregular rhythm against the wall, a sound like tapping fingers. A sound like waiting.

My room is small. Bare.

A cot, a desk, a dim lamp that flickers every time someone turns on a generator two floors up. I've lived in worse places, but somehow this room feels... louder.

Maybe because it's the first time I've been alone since my mother died.

I sit at the desk, datapad open, blank directive screen glowing too bright against the dark. I've been here for an hour—maybe more—trying to force the words that used to come so easily.

"Rally the East Quarter."

"Strike the shipments on the 14th."

"Control the narrative before Empyrium does."

My mother used to say propaganda was just storytelling with purpose.

A weapon, if you sharpen it right.

I try.

I type three words.

Delete two.

Rearrange the last.

The cursor blinks at me like it's judging.

I lean back in the chair, pressing my fingers to my eyes. I can still hear her voice in this room, telling me to breathe, telling me the world is remade by the hands that dare to guide it.

But I'm not my mother.

I never wanted to be.

I'm just the ghost the rebellion stitched together out of her bones.

The rain-thread drips again.

Four beats.

Pause.

Then two more.

My throat tightens.

The room feels too big and too small all at once—the kind of space that swallows sound but amplifies every thought you're trying not to have.

I glance at the propaganda draft again.

Nothing moves.

I should be working.

I should be leading.

I should be writing the words that keep the rebellion breathing.

But the truth presses against my ribs like a bruise:

There is no one here to see if I fail.

No one here to steady the mask back into place.

No one here to remind me that being human isn't the same as being weak.

My hands drop to my lap.

Fingers curl.

Tremble.

Stop.

The silence stretches long enough that I swear I can hear my heartbeat echo off the concrete.

And then—softly, quietly, like the words crawl out from somewhere deeper than thought—I whisper:

"Mercy is a luxury."

It sounds like something my mother would have said the night she taught me how to lie with my eyes open and my pulse steady.

But the next words feel like mine.

Entirely mine.

"But I still have it."

The admission hangs in the air.

Soft.

Vulnerable.

Dangerous.

I don't know if it's a strength or a flaw.

My mother would say strength.

The generals would say weakness.

The empire would say it's a mistake that gets people killed.

But me?

Sitting alone in this rain-leaking box of a room, the rebellion bleeding at the seams, the world spinning faster than I can brace for—

I think it's the only part of me I recognize anymore.

The only part that feels like it hasn't been carved away by expectation, duty, loss.

The lamp flickers again.

The datapad dims.

My shoulders fold forward, slow, controlled, like I'm bowing to the silence.

Isolation isn't loud.

It settles.

Like dust.

Like memory.

Like the weight of someone's hand that isn't there anymore.

I close the directive draft without saving.

Not tonight.

Tonight, the rebellion can survive without its ghost.

But I can't survive without this—this moment where I let myself feel the ache beneath the armor.

The rain-thread taps again.

Steady.

Insistent.

And for the first time since my mother's death, the silence doesn't swallow me whole.

It just... sits with me.

Unmoving.

Unjudging.

The rain-thread taps again.

I try to match my breathing to it—slow in, slow out—but it stutters.

Jitters.

Breaks.

My hands start shaking before I realize it.

I press my palms flat against my knees, willing the tremor to stop, willing my body to remember obedience, discipline, composure—anything that feels like control.

But the harder I push, the more the edges fray.

My vision blurs.

Not now.

Not here.

Not like this.

I swallow hard, the sound too loud in the cramped room, like it echoes off the concrete walls and comes back sharper.

A breath shivers through me.

Then another.

And the truth—the one I've swallowed for months, buried under orders and masks and the rebellion's desperate dependence on a ghost—cuts up through my ribs like broken glass:

I have never felt this alone.

Not even the night she died.

Because that night, I still had her voice in my ear, whispering that I wasn't done yet.

That she believed in me.

That I could carry what she couldn't anymore.

Now there is no voice.

No hand on my shoulder.

No one who knows the shape of me beneath the titles.

A sound escapes my throat—half breath, half sob—so fragile it feels like it isn't meant to exist.

I curl forward, elbows braced on my thighs, fingers laced behind my neck as if I can hold myself together by force alone.

But I can't.

The first tear hits the floor with a tiny, traitorous patter.

Then another.

My shoulders shake—small, sharp, uncontrollable tremors.

Like the dam finally cracked and the water has nowhere left to go.

I press my forehead to my hands.

"I don't know if I can do this," I choke out, my voice shaking so hard it barely sounds like mine.

The confession tastes like blood.

And truth.

And defeat.

The silence absorbs it without mercy.

Without comfort.

I don't know if I will ever trust anyone again the way I trusted my mother.

The way she trusted me.

The way she saw me—not as a symbol, not as a weapon, but as a person.

A small part of me wonders if that kind of trust only happens once in a lifetime.

If I already lost mine.

If this is all I have left—a ghost in a leaking room, crying alone because there is no one left to witness the fracture.

My breath shudders.

I drag my sleeve across my eyes, but the tears keep coming, slow and relentless.

I curl tighter, letting the grief have me for the first time since my mother's execution.

It hurts.

God, it hurts.

But buried somewhere under the ache—deep enough to doubt, fragile enough to break if I touch it—is a thin thread of something else:

The faintest hope that maybe, someday, someone might see me the way she did.

Someone who isn't here yet.

Someone I haven't met.

Someone who might understand this breach in me without fear or judgment.

Someone whose presence might feel like warmth instead of threat.

But that hope is too small, too distant, too unreal to reach for.

Not tonight.

Tonight I break alone.

And when the shaking finally eases, when the last tear dries on my cheek, all that remains is the silence—heavy, honest, and mine.

Chapter 22: Dominion's Parade

Tiberius

The Upper Spires always smells too clean.

Filtered air, polished steel, flowers genetically engineered to never wilt.

Dominion stands at the balcony's edge, basking in sunlight like a god carved in chrome.

I stand half a step behind him—close enough to imply loyalty, far enough to hide the tension in my jaw.

Crowds roar from the plazas below.

Billboards flash Dominion's face in rotating gold.

Drones hover in precise formation, capturing his every breath.

My father raises his hands, and the city falls silent.

I keep my expression neutral.

Composed.

Weaponized.

But my eyes—

My eyes refuse to obey.

They sweep the crowd, scanning a thousand faces.

And I hate myself for the reason why.

Not for threats.

Not for rebels.

Not for the ghost everyone thinks we hunt.

But for **her**.

I don't let the thought form a name.

I don't even let myself acknowledge the shape of it.

Years of discipline, and still—

Still the memory of the arena bleeds through like a wound that never stitched.

A girl standing defiant in the dust.

Indigo-toned eyes glaring at me like they saw straight through the armor.

A warehouse.

A storm-slick night when shadows hid more truth than light.

A hesitation I should've crushed.

Mercy I should've never allowed.

I tell myself I'm searching for a threat.

For a rebel ghost the Empire fears more than bombs.

But that's a lie.

I'm not scanning for a rebel.

I'm scanning for *her*.

A flicker in the main camera feed catches my eye.

A shutter-blink.

A glitch like a breath caught in a machine's throat.

Something tightens beneath my sternum.

I turn my head—slow, subtle—and look directly into the lens.

For a heartbeat, the world narrows.

No roar of crowds.

No Dominion.

No Empire.

Just the sensation of being... *seen*.

And I don't know why.

I don't know by who.

But it hits with the quiet violence of memory.

Dominion starts speaking.

I don't hear a word.

My thoughts whisper:

If ghosts can burn... maybe they can live.

✦ ☽⋆☾ ✦

Aly

Static crackles across the Undergrid relay screen.

The hacked broadcast flickers—cheap wires, rusted metal, far too many hands jacked into one stolen signal.

Dominion's parade is nothing but smeared light and glitch-shadow.

Axel curses softly as he stabilizes the feed.

Vivian paces behind me.

Half the cell pretends they're watching for intel.

The other half pretends they aren't terrified.

I sit still.

Hood up.

Jaw tight.
Eyes sharp even when I wish they weren't.
I don't want to watch this parade.
I don't want to see Dominion bask in his own rot.
But I'm the Ash Commander.
So I watch.
I always watch.
The camera angle shifts—
And Tiberius Braxton fills the screen.
Even through the distortion, he radiates command.
Precision.
Designed perfection.
The Empire's heir.
But I've known him by another name.
The Ghost of the Empire.
And I don't know why I've kept that to myself all these years—
since the warehouse,
the tavern,
and the arena where mercy burned through his restraint.
I should've told Vivian.
Axel.
My mother.
Anyone.
But something in me never let the words leave my throat.
He stands beside Dominion, but he doesn't move like a loyal son.
He moves like a blade held too tightly.
And then—
I notice his eyes.
He isn't scanning the crowd like a soldier.
He's searching.
For something specific.
Someone specific.
A chill climbs my spine.
Axel leans in, muttering, "Feed's glitching, hold—"
The screen fractures—pixel shards and white noise—

—and for one impossible heartbeat, Tiberius Braxton looks *straight at the camera.*

Straight through the glitch.

Straight at **me**.

My pulse stutters.

A trick of timing.

A glitch in the feed.

A coincidence in a collapsing network.

It *has* to be.

But it feels like recognition.

My breath leaves in a quiet, involuntary tremor.

I lean closer, whispering before I can stop myself:

"If ghosts can bleed... maybe they can burn."

The feed snaps back.

Dominion speaks.

The parade roars.

The Empire preens.

The room keeps moving around me.

But the shiver beneath my ribs stays anchored like a hook.

Because for the first time—

watching the Empire from a shadowed corner of the Undergrid—

it feels like someone inside the machine is looking back.

And I don't know if that terrifies me...

or warns me. Or calls to me.

Part III

Inheritance of Ghosts

"Every empire leaves ghosts behind. Some become warnings. Others become weapons."

—Ash Network, File 3C

Chapter 23: Ghost Circuits

Tiberius · Age 28

Sector Six hums like a heart with no pulse.

Screens glow.

Cables breathe.

Machines whisper secrets no one living should hear.

This is where the Empire hides what it doesn't want to admit exists—

glitches, shadows, ghosts in the wires.

I drag a finger down the encrypted Continuum logs, following a pattern that shouldn't be there.

Dominion calls it "sympathizer interference."

He's convinced rebels are clawing at the Directorate's walls again.

He's wrong.

This isn't rebellion work.

It's too clean.

Too deliberate.

Too quiet.

Almost... surgical.

A hesitation-beat flickers in the code—light enough it should be invisible.

But I feel it.

A pull.

A wrongness.

A familiarity I don't want to acknowledge.

My throat tightens before I can stop it.

No.

I shut the reaction down.

Fast.

Efficient.

I'm twenty-eight.

Security General.

Dominion's son.

A weapon no one but him and his council knows about. A living weapon the Empire pretends is just an officer.

I don't get haunted.

I don't imagine patterns.

I don't think about—

Her.

The girl I refused to kill at sixteen.

The same girl who spared me in the arena at eighteen.

The silhouette that disappeared into neon and shadow a decade ago and never surfaced.

Ten years.

Twelve years, if I'm being honest with myself.

I shouldn't remember any of that.

Yet some part of me—reflex, instinct, something bone-deep—reacts to certain signatures in ways I can't explain.

As if my instincts cataloged her long before my mind dared to.

I force my attention back to the console.

The anomaly pulses again.

Soft. Precise.

Like a breath held on purpose.

My jaw tightens.

Not this.

Not now.

I reroute the data through a filtration loop.

It doesn't disperse.

It waits.

It watches.

It feels like someone is inside the system—someone patient enough to slip between lines, someone skilled enough to erase their presence but leave a whisper behind.

Someone who should not be here.

My fingers curl against the desk to ground myself.

It's a hacker.

A sympathizer.

A glitch.

That's what I tell myself.

Not—

—not the girl in the warehouse.

Not the fighter in the arena.

Not the ghost with indigo eyes who has been orbiting the edges of my life since I was sixteen.

I tell myself I barely remember her.

I tell myself I never think about her.

I tell myself I moved on.

The lies come easily.

Practice makes perfect.

Dominion's voice crackles through the overhead speakers.

"Tiberius. Identify the breach."

My pulse doesn't change.

(That's the lie I tell myself next.)

"I'm isolating it now."

"Good. Ghosts breed in hesitation."

The line cuts out.

Hesitation.

Right.

The first thing she ever made me feel.

The anomaly blinks again.

Just once.

Like a heartbeat in the dark.

A ghost-circuit.

A trace from someone who shouldn't exist.

I exhale slowly, locking the tremor in my chest behind discipline where it belongs.

If I name her, she becomes real.

If she's real, she becomes a threat.

If she becomes a threat, Dominion will find her.

So I bury the thought.

The instinct.

The ghost.

And a quieter thought slips through before I can stop it:

What if she never left the system at all?

What if she's been here—just out of reach—the whole time?

I shut it down.

I quarantine the anomaly, strip metadata, shred timestamps until the record is nothing but static and dust.

The screen flickers—like a heartbeat trying to restart—then flatlines.

Clean.

Gone.

Erased.

Exactly what the Empire expects from me.

I lift my hand to press DELETE on the last fragment.

It should be routine.

Mechanical.

Thoughtless.

But my finger hesitates.

A single breath of stillness.

My hand shakes—barely, but enough that I curl it into a fist to hide it from the cameras.

I force the command through.

DELETE.

The anomaly disappears.

But the tremor stays—

the same one that's lived in my bones for twelve years.

A recognition.

A memory.

A ghost I can't erase.

Chapter 24: Missing Transports

Aly · Age 28

The Undergrid tunnels sweat in the summer heat.

Pipes rattle overhead like bones knocking together.

Condensation drips down the concrete walls in slow, uneven beats.

The air tastes like decay, metal, and old secrets—too many of them buried under a city that pretends it doesn't have a basement.

Three years of this.

Three years of being the ghost the rebellion needed, not the person I was allowed to be.

Axel's voice crackles over the comm.

"Convoy Four still hasn't checked in. That makes three this month."

Three Nullborn transports.

Three whole groups of people the Empire claims don't exist.

Once, that thought would've hit me like a punch.

Now it lands lower—deeper—in the part of me that's tired of choosing who to save first.

I drag my hand across a steel support beam—cool, damp, trembling ever so slightly with the pulse of the city above us.

The vibration feels wrong.

The silence feels worse.

Kai stands a few paces back, impatience radiating off him like static.

"This is a waste of time, Commander."

I feel my jaw tighten at the title.

I never wanted it.

It was shoved into my hands the night my mother died, and no matter how tightly I've gripped it, it keeps cutting deeper.

"We should be focusing on the governor race," he continues. "The East District is vulnerable. One wrong move and the whole political chain collapses."

Vivian scoffs, crossing her arms.

"People are disappearing and you want Aly to worry about votes?"

Kai's jaw ticks.

"Convoys go missing. This is the Undergrid. That's nothing new."

"Three in a month," I say quietly.

He doesn't answer.

Vivian steps closer, voice sharp as broken glass.

"We expose this. We leak everything. A full broadcast. Names, numbers, transport routes—"

"No," I cut in.

Both of them whirl to me.

Vivian looks wounded.

Kai looks relieved—almost smug.

I kneel beside the rail, brushing grime away with the back of my hand.

Faint tire grooves.

Too light for military.

Too clean for smugglers.

Someone tried to hide them but didn't know the patterns this deep.

"They didn't run," I say. "They were taken."

Vivian's breath hitches.

Kai exhales hard. "Even if you're right—if someone's targeting Nullborn lines—we gain nothing by chasing ghosts. We gain ground by moving up, not down."

There it is.

The quiet rot I've been pretending I don't see.

I rise, slowly.

"Nullborn aren't leverage," I say. "They're people."

My voice is steady.

Cold, even.

But inside, a part of me flinches—because saying it aloud makes the role crack again, just a little.

Tired.

Too tired.

Kai holds my gaze, waiting for me to back down.

Waiting for me to choose the command mask over the person beneath it.

"Compassion doesn't win wars," he says.

"No," I reply, "but cruelty loses them."

Vivian's eyes shine for a beat—hope, gratitude, rebellion.

Kai's face shutters.

"You need to think bigger," he pushes.

I breathe in slow, through the fatigue, through the weight I never asked for.

"I am," I say. "But bigger doesn't mean colder."

He steps back like I hit him.

Vivian exclaims softly under her breath.

When Kai turns and storms down the tunnel, the tension follows him like smoke.

Vivian glances at me, voice quieter.

"You're exhausted."

I don't deny it.

Leadership was never my calling—just the only option left.

If I take off the mask, everything collapses.

If I keep wearing it, I will.

"Do you think they're being erased?" she asks.

I look down the tunnel—into the dark, into the hum, into the place where the Empire hides the things it's most afraid of.

"People," I say. "Records. Whole histories."

A beat.

"Someone is removing them."

Vivian swallows hard.

"Why?"

I don't have the answer.

But something in the shadows feels familiar—a rhythm beneath the static, a pulse in the circuits, the same quiet, surgical wrongness I've felt before.

And in the back of my mind:

If the Empire is erasing people... What else has already been erased?

I turn toward the deeper tunnels.

"Prep the team," I tell Vivian. "I'm going in alone first."

She hesitates—one heartbeat—then nods.

She understands.

Some paths must be walked by a ghost.

And some burdens must be carried by the person the world refuses to let be human.

I lift my hood.

Step into the dark.

And the tunnels breathe around me like they're hiding a truth waiting to swallow me whole.

Chapter 25: Beneath the Ion Veil

Tiberius

The Ion Veil vibrates through the tower floor—steady, mechanical, alive in the way engineered systems are when too many people depend on them.

Sector Six's observation deck is quiet.

It always is.

Up here, noise is a distraction, and distraction is unacceptable.

I scan the console's diagnostics:

Unauthorized transmissions.

Minor breaches.

Low-level signal drift.

Dominion expects me to flag everything.

The Directorate expects me to crush everything.

But none of this is rebellion work.

Not the real kind.

This pattern—this cadence in the code—is too precise.

Too deliberate.

Almost elegant.

A fragment of encryption flickers on the screen.

Not quite old rebellion code.

Not quite Directorate format.

Something in between.

A hybrid.

I narrow my eyes and lean in.

This isn't noise.

This isn't amateur hacking.

This is someone testing the boundaries of the grid.

Someone who knows what they're doing.

Someone who learned to move quietly inside systems built to catch everything.

My pulse stays steady.

Professionally.

Predictably.

But something under the surface... shifts.

Not recognition.

Not memory.

Reflex.

Like the way a muscle remembers an injury long after it heals.

I shut the thought down.

Hard.

Twelve years ago is irrelevant.

Ten years ago is irrelevant.

Nothing from that period has operational value now.

And whoever she was—

(if she even existed outside adrenaline and poor visibility)

—she isn't my concern.

This code is.

I dissect the fragment, tracing its path through the Ion Veil's layered architecture. It bypasses Dominion's primary filters, skirts the Continuum firewalls, then dissipates without leaving a trace.

Smart.

Not perfect.

But close.

Too close.

I should report it.

Protocol is clear.

But protocol also assumes the Directorate is stable.

After three months of internal discrepancies, I'm not convinced.

Dominion blames sympathizers.

The data suggests internal manipulation.

If I forward this anomaly, it goes straight into hands I no longer trust without verification.

My fingers hover over the command line.

A simple choice:

Flag.

Or follow.

I reroute the fragment into a private encrypted cache.

It isn't rebellion.

Not yet.

It's a question.

One I want the answer to before my father gets his hands on it.

The console hums, waiting for my report.

I open the interface, ready to enter the standard:

"*No actionable breach detected.*"

My hand hesitates.

Not for long.

A second.

A breath.

Small enough no one watching the feed would notice.

But I notice.

My finger taps the key.

The report sends.

Efficient.

Unremarkable.

Proper.

I lock my private cache and step back from the console, watching the Ion Veil pulse along the city's spine.

Somewhere inside that grid, someone is moving with precision.

With intent.

With skill.

Someone dangerous.

Someone familiar only in the way a pattern is familiar once you've studied it too many times.

I exhale once, controlled and even.

"Ghosts," Dominion likes to say, "are born from failure."

Maybe.

But this one feels like it's born from design.

And whatever it is—

I intend to find it before anyone else does.

Chapter 26: The Contact

Aly

The meeting chamber reeks of ion dust and tarnished heat pipes—

exactly the kind of place where hope comes to die.

Smugglers mill around the edges, half shadows, half rumors.

Kai stands in the doorway like he owns the room, arms crossed, smile thin enough to cut.

I don't sit.

Commanders sit when they want to look comfortable.

I haven't felt comfortable in three years.

Vivian slips in behind me, muttering, "If he starts talking in circles again, I'm hitting him."

I ignore her.

Because Kai never calls these meetings unless he wants something...

or someone wants something from us.

"Commander," he starts, with a bow just deep enough to be insulting, "we've intercepted coordinates. A sympathizer inside the Empire."

A snort rises in the room. Nobody believes in sympathizers.

I don't either.

Not anymore.

"Coordinates for what?" I ask.

Kai taps his wrist-brace. A holo flickers to life—grid numbers, time stamps, a restricted Dominion chain of custody.

Sublevel Data Vault access markers.

My pulse stumbles—just once, then steadies, cold and hard.

He keeps talking. Something about risk, timing, leverage. I barely hear him.

Because three years ago, before my mother died she whispered one thing to me. Her final order to me:

'You find my file. All of it. Everything on me. You erase it. Every trace. Promise me.'

I promised.

I never told anyone.

Not Kai.

Not Axel.

Not Vivian.

Not any of the other generals.

Just me.

For three years, I've been chasing ghosts through fractured channels, half-broken systems, erased histories—

searching for a crack in the Empire big enough to slip through.

And now Kai stands here offering coordinates tied to the one place I've never been able to reach.

I narrow my eyes.

"Why now?"

He smiles. Too neat. Too confident.

"Because someone inside wants to help you."

A lie.

Or a trap.

Or both.

Vivian shifts beside me. "Aly... this feels wrong."

Everything feels wrong.

My reflection in the cracked steel wall looks like a commander I never wanted to be—tired eyes, tightened jaw, mask that's starting to crumble around the edges.

I remember the riots.

The faces I failed.

The ghosts I carry.

My mother's last breath.

And the last two times the Empire's shadows brushed mine—a warehouse door scraping shut, an arena trembling with fire, a glitching parade feed where someone on a balcony looked straight through a camera and into my bones.

Ghost circuits.

Patterns that don't belong.

I swallow once, steady.

"If this is a trap," I say quietly, "it's a well-made one."

Vivian whispers, "Then don't go."

I lift my chin.

"I'm going."

Kai smirks like he expected nothing else.

I step closer, eyes locked on the coordinates burning blue in the dim room.

"If these lead where I think they lead," I murmur, "then the Empire's been hiding more than files."

Three years of searching.

Three years of walls.

And now, finally—a door.

Hope. Small. Dangerous. Exhausting.

But still hope.

And if it kills me?

So be it.

"Send the coordinates to my private line," I say.

"I'll walk into it myself."

Kai's smile sharpens.

Vivian's hand tightens on my arm.

And somewhere in the wires, in a part of the system I can't name—something watches back.

Chapter 27: Market of Masks

Aly

The Neon Markets never sleep. Why would it? I have never known it to.

Light spills in fractured colors across metal stalls—pink, cyan, indigo washing over a hundred faces that could all be mine, if I let myself pretend. Synthetic incense burns thick in the air. Voices crash together in a river of noise.

Perfect for a disguise.

Perfect for lies.

Vivian's voice crackles in my ear:

"In and out. Don't get sentimental."

As if I have any sentiment left.

My hood shadows most of my face, but not the exhaustion. That sits in my bones no matter how tightly I wrap myself.

I slide between vendors, trading coded phrases, covert tokens, old rebel markers. My hands move automatically. My mind... not so much.

Three years wearing masks, and this one feels heavier than all the others.

I didn't become a commander.

I was cornered into the role.

Now every step in these tunnels feels like someone else's path, someone else's life, someone else's destiny sewn onto my skin.

Vivian would call this paranoia.

Kai would call it weakness.

But I feel it.

A pressure.

A shift in the air.

Like a storm trying to form inside metal walls.

A flickering neon sign leads me to the trader I need.

A man with glass eyes and a soft, artificial voice.

"You're late," he says.

"I'm alive," I answer. "That's early."

He snorts, hands over a sliver-chip wrapped in old encryption cloth.

The clearance chain glows faintly.

Vault-tier signature.

My fingers tremble—barely—but he notices anyway.

"You sure you want to look inside that tomb, girl?"

Girl.

I almost correct him—Commander—but the word tastes wrong.

"I don't want to," I say.

"But I have to."

My mother's last order burns under my ribs:

Erase my file.

Erase the truth before they twist it.

I tuck the chip into my sleeve and move into the thicker part of the crowd.

And that's when **it** happens.

A brush.

A shoulder against mine—firm, solid, warm through fabric.

Not accidental.

Not intentional.

Just... inevitable.

Something electric jumps beneath my skin.

I don't look up.

I can't.

My instincts whisper **danger**.

Another part of me whispers something closer to **memory**.

I hold my breath.

The crowd swallows the moment whole.

I force myself forward, deeper into lights and smoke and voices I don't trust.

But something in my chest flares—a heartbeat like a warning,

or recognition, or both.

I swallow hard and keep walking.

I don't look back.

Because I can't afford to.

Because if I do—

I might not be able to stop.

I keep walking.

But something fragile trembles under my ribs—as if I already know I should've looked back.

✦ ☽⋆☾ ✦

Tiberius

Sector Three of the Neon Markets is a myth wrapped in electricity.

Too many bodies.

Too many feeds.

Too many blind spots where trouble grows like mold.

My father calls this place a "cesspit."

I call it a map of Empire rot.

I'm here on official inspection—but really, I'm here for something else.

The anomaly from Sector Six.

It doesn't leave me alone.

Not in the circuits,

not in my instincts,

not in the quiet between breaths.

A pattern threaded through years of data.

A whisper.

A signal.

A ghost.

One I refuse to acknowledge.

I move through the market with precision—scanning faces, scanning feeds, scanning anything that might hint at the breach source. The Directorate wants answers. My father wants control.

I want the truth before either of them get it.

I'm good at burying distractions.

At thirty steps a minute, I can compartmentalize almost anything.

Something tightens low in my spine—a subtle pull, like a thread tugged by unseen hands.

An instinct I shouldn't trust.

A memory I shouldn't have.

I push through a cluster of people shifting around a vendor stall.

And then—

I collide with someone.

Just a shoulder, a step, a slip of space—but it hits like static crawling over my ribs.

My breath stutters.

I don't turn.

I can't.

Logic orders me forward.

Protocol demands I keep my eyes moving.

Duty requires I ignore anything that doesn't present itself as threat.

But—

Something brushes against me in the crowd and the world narrows to a pinpoint.

A scent—clean ozone, faint smoke.

A movement—quick, practiced.

A presence—familiar in a way that twists something deep and old inside my ribs.

For half a second, the marketplace noise fades.

Data feeds blur.

Training fractures.

I swallow.

I don't look back.

Because the last time I followed a feeling like this—it rewrote the trajectory of my life.

And because if it's *her*—

No.

Not now.

Not again.

Not until I know.

My hand lifts, almost of its own accord, brushing the air between us as if the moment could still be caught.

But there's nothing there.

Just the crowd.

Just the Markets.

Just a ghost.

A ghost my instincts learned long before I ever understood why.

I force myself forward, voice steady, expression iron.

But my pulse—

My pulse lies through its teeth.

And as the crowd swallows both of us, something tightens in my jaw—like a recognition without memory.

Like a name I don't know yet.

Like a ghost circuit waking up.

I exhale slow, controlled.

If that was anything real, I'll find it again.

If it wasn't... then I'll kill the part of me that hoped it was.

I move on.

But the pull in my chest does not.

It echoes.

Almost like a heartbeat.

Almost like a warning.

Almost like someone walking away with something of mine I never meant to give.

Chapter 28: Dominion's Command

Tiberius

The council chamber feels colder today.

Not temperature—Dominion controls that down to the micro degree—but **atmosphere**.

Tension slicks across the polished obsidian floor like oil.

Dominion stands at the head of the table, hands clasped behind his back.

He doesn't look at the councilors.

He looks *through* them.

A sign I know well.

He's already decided something none of them will like.

"Efficiency in the lower sectors has dropped twelve percent," he says, voice smooth as glass. "Discontent breeds infection. Infection must be burned out."

Councilor Mereth swallows.

Councilor Jarrow shifts in his seat.

No one breathes deeply.

I register movement by the door:

Grey, posted on guard rotation.

Back straight.

Expression neutral.

Eyes forward.

Dominion turns.

"Sector purge. Two tiers. Immediate."

A silence drops so heavy it almost cracks the floor.

A purge means:

families displaced,

supply lines severed,

fear weaponized

until the streets forget what hope tastes like.

It also means rebellion spreads faster, not slower.

Dominion knows this.

He doesn't care.

I keep my expression neutral.

I have worn neutrality like armor since I was a boy.

"Father," I say, stepping just slightly forward—the exact distance that's acceptable for 'advisory input' without appearing insolent. "Lower sectors are already strained. A purge at this scale risks destabilizing production altogether."

Dominion's eyes narrow.

Not anger.

Calculation.

"Production?" he repeats.

"Food units. Energy grids. Textile for winter distribution," I answer calmly. "If you remove two tiers, the system collapses faster than it recovers. You'll lose three months of output."

A murmur passes through the council.

I continue, tone steady, almost bored:

"A controlled recalibration protocol will motivate compliance without compromising infrastructure. A strategic squeeze, not a cut."

This is how you rebel when you live under a tyrant's shadow:

You weaponize reason.

You sharpen logic until it becomes a shield.

You let obedience sound like strategy.

Dominion studies me for a long, surgical moment.

"Tiberius," he finally says, voice soft. "You hesitate."

My pulse clicks once, a single hitch under the ribs.

I don't blink.

"I calculate," I correct gently. "Hesitation is emotional. Calculation is efficient."

He likes that answer.

Of course he does.

Emotion is weakness.

Logic is loyalty.

That's what he believes.

He steps closer, placing a hand on my shoulder—a gesture that means nothing but dominance.

"Then calculate well," he murmurs. "Keep your innovators alive. We will proceed with your... 'recalibration.'"

A moment passes.

"Two weeks. No more."

I bow my head.

"Yes, sir."

Councilors exhale.

The tension loosens enough for them to breathe again.

Dominion moves on, issuing orders about weapons testing and propaganda cycles.

I stand still.

Externally: calm.

Internally: cataloging every consequence I just prevented, and every new crack exposing the empire's rot.

A purge postponed is still a purge, just slower.

A problem deferred.

A cruelty delayed.

But I bought thousands of people two weeks.

Two weeks can shift a rebellion.

Two weeks can save a transport.

Two weeks can hide a ghost.

I don't think of her.

Not consciously.

Not deliberately.

But some part of me does anyway—that instinctual place where memory and defiance share a pulse.

I file the purge order under "restricted," reroute it through three non-traceable nodes, and schedule a mandatory review in exactly thirteen days.

A bureaucratic snarl.

A knot in the empire's spine.

Dominion would call it efficiency.

I know better.

This is rebellion in its quietest form.

A small, silent "no" hidden inside a perfect "yes."

I turn to exit the chamber, shoulders squared, steps measured.

As I pass the guards, Grey doesn't move—doesn't break formation—doesn't even shift his gaze from the wall.

But—

the corner of his mouth twitches.

A fractional smile.

Gone in an instant.

Too small for Dominion.

Too disciplined for the council.

But not too small for me.

It means:

I saw what you did. I agree. Keep going.

I don't look at him.

I don't acknowledge it.

But as I step through the doors, the cold of the chamber lifts just slightly.

Because someone in this place still remembers how to be human.

And someone else just silently told me:

You're not alone.

If I ever need to save someone the empire wants erased, this is how I'll do it—

slow, careful, invisible rebellion, hidden inside obedience.

Chapter 29: Inheritance of Ghosts

Aly

My quarters aren't really quarters.

Just a metal box carved into the Undergrid ribs, lit by a single strip of failing blue light.

Enough space for a cot, a desk, and the ghosts I pretend I don't carry.

Tonight, they feel heavier.

The chipped relay screen flickers as I pull up the encrypted file the smuggler traded me.

The coordinates Kai delivered.

The "sympathizer tip."

The access chain that shouldn't exist.

And the file it leads to:

Transfer 42-B.

My mother's designation.

Lara Carmichael.

My stomach knots.

I shouldn't even have a right to this file.

Only high-ranking Directorate historians and Dominion's inner circle would ever see anything tied to Lara.

And yet—here it is.

Surface-level, locked in a static cage of encryption.

Just enough to let me know it exists.

Not enough to open it.

Just enough to hurt.

The displayed text is bare, clinical:

LARA CARMICHAEL—TRANSFER 42-B

Status: *Rebel leader*

Crime: *High treason*

Outcome: *Execution by Empyrium Decree*

That's all the Undergrid gets.

All anyone gets.

But there are deeper sections—layered beneath the surface text like bones beneath skin.

Sections I can see but not access:

42-B/III – Bloodline Registry

42-B/V – Pre-Dominion Governance History

42-B/X – Offspring Clearance: Unconfirmed

42-B/XII – Suppressed Ancestral Record

42-B/XIV – Legacy Risk Assessment: CONFIDENTIAL

My pulse stumbles.

Bloodline.

Suppressed.

Legacy.

Offspring unconfirmed.

I stare at the screen too long, until the light vibrates against the edges of my skull.

No one in the rebellion ever talked about Lara's lineage.

Most of my generals weren't alive when she started all this.

Those who were never spoke of bloodlines or rulership or the old council families.

All they knew was that Lara Carmichael lit the first match,

and Dominion crushed her for it.

And they never knew she had a daughter.

No one does.

My mother never told me much about her life before the rebellion.

Just fragments.

Shadows.

Pieces she let slip when she forgot to guard her voice.

I know she was only eighteen when I was born—but she'd already been fighting for two years by then.

Already a symbol.

Already hunted.

Once, when I was young, I asked her about my father.

She went very still.

Then she gave me this soft, far-off look I didn't understand at the time—equal parts ache and memory—and she whispered, "*He was the love of my life, Aly.*"

Nothing more.

I asked again.

And again.

She never answered.

But I grew up watching her expression whenever his shadow crossed her thoughts.

I learned to read the silence she carried like a wound.

Two years ago, I finally pieced it together.

Found him.

Spoke to him for all of ten minutes.

He didn't know who I was.

I didn't tell him.

For my safety.

For the rebellion's.

And—if I'm honest—for his.

Some truths become targets the moment you name them.

So I walked away with the answers I needed
and the ones I couldn't afford to give.

Thirty years of history rewritten.

Thirty years of silence.

Thirty years of burying me—even from myself.

And Dominion's archive still kept her file alive.

Still kept *this*.

I grip the edge of the desk until my knuckles go white.

My mother's last order echoes in the hollow of my chest, the way it's echoed for the last three years:

"You find my file. All of it. Everything on me. You erase it. Every trace."

I swallow hard, throat tight.

I haven't spoken those words aloud in decades.

Never told Vivian.

Never told Kai.

Never told Axel.

Never told anyone.

Because if I did?

Someone would ask the question I can't afford:

Why would a rebel commander give her daughter an order meant for a ruler's heir?

I close the file.

The blue light flickers once—like a pulse.

The truth is simple:

I can't erase these records from here.

The access chain only leads to the Data Vault.

The real Data Vault.

The one buried under the Citadel—the one Dominion believes no rebel could ever reach.

But I will.

Even if it kills me.

Because if my mother's truth is in there—if her *real* history is in there; if any trace of who she was or what she protected still exists—I can't leave it in the Empire's hands.

I lean back, exhaustion sinking into the marrow.

This isn't just duty.

Or rebellion.

Or command.

This is hers.

The last thing she ever gave me.

And the last thing she ever asked of me.

My voice is barely a whisper in the metal room:

"I'll finish it, Mom. I'll erase you myself."

But as I shut down the screen, a quieter thought curls under my ribs—

What if the Empire didn't keep her file to bury her?

What if they kept it to bury something *else*?

And for the first time in years, I am afraid of the truth waiting for me in the Data Vault.

Chapter 30: The Descent

Aly

The Undergrid sleeps in fragments.

A generator stutters somewhere behind the safehouse wall. Pipes groan like old bones settling. The neon strips that serve as night-lights flicker in and out, making the shadows pulse in slow breaths. Everyone here sleeps with a weapon under their pillow or their hand curled around someone else's.

I wait until the last whisper dies.

Kai's door has stopped glowing.

Vivian's music finally cut out.

Even Axel—usually a restless night-walker—is quiet.

Good.

I pull my boots on silently, lacing them tight, and sling my jacket over my shoulders. My hood comes up, shadowing my face. A flare of guilt tries to spark, but I crush it. If any of them knew where I was going, I'd have an entire squad blocking the door. Or worse—following me.

This is something I need to do alone.

For once... without a witness.

Without the weight of their loyalty breathing down my neck.

The tunnels breathe cold air as I step into them. They smell like oxidation and wet stone, like secrets stewing in the dark. My footsteps echo too loudly, so I adjust my gait until I'm almost gliding, body attuned to the hush—becoming the hush.

The farther I walk, the more the air changes.

The grit thins.

The stink of oil fades.

The hum of battered machines turns into something smoother, higher—like a city exhaling only when it knows the poor aren't watching.

And then I reach the ramp that leads upward.

The Undergrid ends abruptly. The upper city begins like a lie wrapped in light.

I pull my hood off my head and slip into the night, letting the cold blue glow wash over me. It feels like stepping into someone else's dream.

The streets up here glow soft blue—not the harsh neon of the slums, but a polished, curated glow meant to soothe the elite into compliance. Security drones float overhead, scanning patterns that never quite dip low enough to catch me. The walkways are clean. Too clean. The air doesn't taste like metal—just cold, filtered nothingness.

No one stops me.

No one even looks at me.

Up here, the Empire has trained them not to see the ghosts of the gutter.

A fresh ache pulls tight under my ribs.

Some part of me will always belong to the dark I crawled out of.

I reach the gleaming spine of the citadel, towering like a blade stabbed into the center of the city. The glass plating catches the moonlight, carving it into sharp geometry. My palm sweats as I touch the concealed panel.

The clearance string digs into my wrist where I hid it.

The scanner pulses... accepts.

The door exhales open.

And I step into the Empyrium Data Vault alone.

Tiberius

The alert hits my comm like a needle to the spine.

"INTRUDER DETECTED—LEVEL SEVEN—SECTOR NINE."

Sector Nine.

The Citadel.

The archives.

No one breaks into the Data Vault.

No one even *thinks* about breaking into it.

It's death by design.

My blood chills.

I'm halfway down the barracks hall before I register moving, boots striking too sharply against the polished floor. The night cycle lighting paints everything in deep blue—same shade as those damn purge lights. My pulse thrums with the same mechanical tempo.

Ghosts.

Every alarm feels like ghosts trying to drag themselves back into my hands.

"Commander Braxton," a synthetic voice crackles. "Proceed to the descent platform immediately."

I grit my teeth and push harder.

The lift platform looms ahead—metal, glass, metal again, all of it humming with the familiar undercurrent of Dominion's design. I step inside and the walls seal around me.

The elevator hum begins its low vibration.

That sound.

It's the same note that lives under my helmet speakers, under my heartbeat, under the silence of every execution chamber I've walked out of alive. It's the sound of being lowered into something you can't climb back out of.

As it descends toward the lower tiers of the citadel, the voice repeats:

"Level Seven intrusion. Unknown identity. Extreme caution advised."

Unknown.

Someone good enough to get past the outer gates.

Someone desperate enough to try.

A strange prickle slides down the back of my neck—familiar, but I can't place why. The hum deepens as the elevator drops, a resonance that sits too close to my bones.

I breathe out once.

Steady.

Whoever this intruder is... they're already below.

And I'm coming straight down the same path they took.

Parallel lines.

Two trajectories on a collision course.

Neither of us seeing the other yet.

But the hum keeps rising, like the city itself knows what's about to happen.

Part IV

Names Like Fire

"Some names burn themselves into history—others ignite the moment they meet. Spoken in fear they crumble into ash; spoken in awe they rise as fire."

Chapter 31: Ghost Entry

Aly

The lift exhales behind me as it seals shut, leaving me in a corridor of glass, stone, and silence sharp enough to cut.

Sector Nine's inner access causeway stretches ahead like the spine of the citadel—long, cold, gleaming. Too empty. Too watchful. The kind of place where sound feels hunted.

The floor reflects the pale blue overhead strips, turning the space into a tunnel of twin ghosts: me above, me below.

Two versions of myself moving in perfect sync—one real, one the thing this place wants me to become.

I pull a slow breath, steadying myself.

Now comes the dangerous part.

This level is guarded by rotating biometric gates—the ones Dominion had installed after the Carmichael Incident, something I was told about but never witnessed. They don't just read your clearance string. They read you. Pulse, thermal patterns, micro-muscle tension, even the cadence of your steps.

The system doesn't just detect intruders.

It profiles fear.

I walk forward anyway.

The first gate recognizes the clearance string, bathing my wrist in soft white light.

ACCESS VERIFIED—PROCEED.

I pass through without hesitation, though my throat tightens as the gate seals behind me with a hiss like a predator satisfied.

But the next two gates tighten the air. Their sensors flicker amber before they settle on white again. Amber means suspicion. Amber means the system is thinking too long about me—tasting the edges of my heartbeat.

Too long is fatal.

I adjust my breathing to the shallow pattern—low pulse, minimal thoracic expansion. Undergrid trick. It makes you read faint, almost flat, like someone half-sedated.

Someone who doesn't pose a threat.

Someone not worth remembering.

Gate Three clears me.

Gate Four is the problem.

Its sensor scans down my arm, pauses over the thin clearance tag strapped around my wrist—the one I received just weeks ago. The one I shouldn't have. The one that marks me as belonging somewhere I never have.

The light wavers.

Amber.

White.

Amber again.

My stomach drops.

A bead of cold sweat slides between my shoulder blades, caught instantly by the chill in the air.

A guard stationed beside the gate straightens, hand drifting toward the holster on his thigh. His visor cants in my direction, scanning my outline.

His fingers hover, tense, patient—trained to shoot before a heartbeat finishes.

Not yet.

Not yet.

Not here.

I shift my wrist just slightly—just enough that the tag catches the sensor at a different angle, forcing a tiny delay. A micro-lag. Something I learned slipping past market scanners in the Undergrid.

The scanner freezes for one breath.

One breath too long.

Then—

ACCESS VERIFIED.

The guard's visor dims.

His hand drops back to rest.

His attention slides off me like I'm not worth the bandwidth to log.

I keep walking.

Don't speed up.

Don't look back.

Don't acknowledge the near miss sitting like lead in your lungs.

I've lived my whole life unseen.

Being seen now would kill me.

The causeway narrows ahead, funneling into a dim sector where the walls are thicker, darker—reinforced. The hum of the citadel changes here, deepening, like a heartbeat buried beneath stone.

The air changes again, colder and more metallic, as though the citadel knows I'm approaching something I shouldn't.

As though the walls themselves draw a breath and hold it.

My boots hit the next strip of polished stone.

A calm settles over me—not soft, but honed, a blade pulled from its sheath.

I finish this

or I stop pretending.

No more half-truths.

No more hiding in the wake of everyone else's bravery.

No more waiting for someone stronger to clear the path.

I move down the final stretch of corridor, pulse steady, footfalls silent, body aligned with the shadows and reflections. My outline fragments across the glass walls, splitting me into shards—each one a version of who I could've been if I wasn't born on the wrong side of the city.

For the first time in my life, I understand the advantage of being overlooked.

Of being quiet.

Of being no one.

I'm not invisible.

I'm impossible to track.

A ghost in plain sight.

And the citadel doesn't even know I'm already inside its heart.

Chapter 32: Countermeasure

Tiberius

The security junction sits like a nerve cluster beneath the Vault—warm, humming, overbright. A place designed for precision, not people. Every surface reflects movement. Every console is a vein feeding Dominion's eyes.

I step inside and the door seals behind me with a metallic lock-click that feels too final.

ANOMALY DETECTED—LEVEL SEVEN.

BREACH ROUTE: 42-B SUB-LEVEL.

The text scrolls across the primary holo-screen in violent red.

My pulse doesn't spike.

It tightens—like a fist curling around a blade.

Level Seven in the Data Vault means one of two responses:

1. Trigger purge protocol.

2. Isolate the breach manually.

One kills everything in the affected hall—personnel, files, systems, air.

Dominion prefers that option. It's his answer to unpredictability.

The other contains the intruder long enough to identify them, assess motive, and preserve what's in the Vault.

My training demands the purge.

But something colder, older, deeper—something that recognizes the echo of familiarity in the breach path—tells me not to.

I pull up the sub-grid map.

A thin route pulses red:

ENTRY: Transfer Hall

DELTA-PATH: 42-B

CURRENT POSITION: ACTIVE TERMINAL

Someone is *still there.*

Not running.

Not flailing.

Working.

A ghost with purpose.

My hand hovers over the purge command.

One touch.

One breath.

A thousand tons of pressure vents and wipes the place clean.

My breathing stays even, but the mask slips for a fraction of a second—just long enough for something close to instinct to break through.

Purge is the wrong call.

Too loud.

Too final.

Too much like the old days, when I didn't question anything.

I flick to manual override.

The system hesitates, surprised. No one chooses this path. Not unless Dominion orders it.

"Authorization required," the AI intones.

"Isolate breach protocol delays execution by fifteen minutes. Confirm?"

Fifteen minutes is the difference between murder and truth.

Between routine obedience and something... else.

"Commander Braxton," the AI prompts again.

"Confirm?"

My jaw locks.

Control, once a shield, settles into a choice.

"...Isolate it."

My voice comes out low, steady. "Authorization Braxton-Tiberius-01."

The AI processes.

The red warning dims to amber.

BREACH ISOLATED.

SECTOR SEALED.

PURGE PROTOCOL SUSPENDED.

Systems reroute.

Doors lock into place.

Airflow diverts.

Every exit leading into 42-B hisses shut except one—the one I'm closest to.

Good.

I don't want the intruder dead.

Not yet.

Not by Dominion's hand.

Not by mine unless there's no other choice.

The console hum deepens, echoing through the junction floor and up my spine.

I step back from the screen.

Isolation buys me time.

Time to get answers.

Time to see who broke into the one place no one is stupid—or desperate—enough to breach.

Time to see why something in me recognized their path before I even saw the alert.

The overhead alarm softens to a pulse instead of a scream, rippling quietly in the metal panels.

I exhale once.

Not relief.

Something sharper.

Something I should not be feeling.

Then I turn toward the lift that will carry me down to sub-lever seven.

Toward the intruder.

Toward the truth I just chose to protect—

instead of the Empire I'm sworn to serve.

Chapter 33: The Sanctum

Tiberius

The descent platform drops the moment I step in, the doors sealing behind me with that signature hydraulic whisper—too soft to be friendly, too precise to be anything but a warning.

The hum begins immediately.

Low.

Resonant.

Vibrating beneath my boots and up my spine.

I know this sound.

Every soldier in the Empire knows it.

You hear it on your way down before a purge. Before a sentence. Before the silence.

My jaw tightens.

Halfway through the descent, my comm crackles:

"Intruder location updated—Transfer 42-B sub-level. Repeat: 42-B."

42-B.

A pulse of recognition flickers—sharp and instinctive—but I stamp it out.

I know the Data Vault too well. Too many nights running simulations.

Too many clean-up missions after Dominion's quiet purges.

There's a faster route.

The lift reaches Level Seven and I step out without hesitation, turning immediately left instead of right because isolation protocol has sealed every standard access point on this floor.

Only one path remains viable—the one the system leaves open for commanding officers.

I slip through a maintenance door that only commanders and archivists know exists.

The isolation lock keeps every other route dead-bolted, but this one stays open for oversight personnel—exactly as designed.

The narrow passage hums with heat from the data conduits, casting the walls in dull red.

I move quickly.

Through the side hall.

Down the grated steps.

Across the junction with the emergency shutters.

Straight into the chamber behind Console Sector Forty.

My boots hit quiet stone as I emerge into the archive proper—dim, cold, pristine.

And then I see her.

Shoulders tight, braced, silhouetted by the glow of the console.

Fingers poised over the data stream like she's about to peel back the skin of the Empire itself.

There's something about her stance—her breath, the tilt of her head—that sparks a pulse of familiarity deep in my chest.

I crush it instantly.

This is an intruder.

A threat.

A ghost where no ghost should breathe.

But I still don't move.

The hum under the floor deepens, vibrating around the chamber like a held note between us.

She leans forward.

The console flickers.

And I stand there, unseen in the shadows behind her...

Watching.

Watching as the screen opens the secret she came for.

Watching as something in my chest goes very, very still.

I don't speak.

I don't step forward.

I only stare at the intruder reflected in the glass—

—unaware that she has already changed everything.

✦ ☽⋆☾ ✦

Aly

Inside the archive everything gleams.

Polished steel.

Pale white lighting.

A thin band of blue along the floor that pulses in steady intervals like a heartbeat crafted by a machine.

The air feels colder here... or maybe it's the weight of what waits in this room.

I move deeper into Archive D. The silence is thick, heavy, the kind that feels like it's pressing a hand over your mouth. Cooling stacks line the far wall behind the consoles, each one humming at a low, constant frequency. The sound vibrates up through the floor, into my spine—steady, rhythmic, almost alive.

A heartbeat.

Not mine.

I reach Console 42-B.

The number jolts through me like a half-forgotten dream.

Like something whispered to me once when I was too young to understand the danger.

My fingers tremble as I activate the terminal.

The index blooms open—thousands of entries, thousands of losses, each one a life rewritten into Empire-approved fiction.

I scroll.

And scroll.

And then—

There.

TRANSFER FILE: 42-B

ORIGIN: L. CARMICHAEL

ACCESS: CONTINUUM PRIEST-LEVEL

STATUS: REDACTED

Redacted so cleanly the screen barely registers her name before blanking it out.

A breath leaves me too fast.

"Of course he buried you this deep," I whisper.

My mother didn't leave many instructions.

None about this vault.

None about how to break into Dominion's sanctum.

But she did tell me one thing—one thing that kept me awake for years:

"If I disappear... you delete whatever they keep of me. You don't let him own my story."

She asked me to delete her file.

Fine.

Then I'll burn the archive he tried to trap her in.

The main console won't let me in—priest-level clearance might as well be a god-seal. But I know these vault rooms. They're not perfect. Dominion doesn't understand imperfection the way Undergrid people do—how it creates openings.

I spot it:

A side console—maintenance tier. Older. Less armored.

Perfect.

I cross the room and kneel, sliding back the manual service panel with a muted metallic click. My pulse syncs with the hum of the cooling stacks as I pull the fiber lines out, rerouting them into the unsecured port.

The lights on the console flicker.

Twice.

Then stabilize on a raw code interface.

"Sorry, Mom," I breathe. "This is going to get messy."

I type fast—Undergrid shorthand, the kind of command language Dominion's upper ranks never learned to read. A destructive burn script builds across the bottom of the screen, line by line, forming the red tide that will wipe 42-B clean.

If I time the execution window right, I can reach her file before the security kernel fights back.

The cooling stacks hum louder.

Deeper.

In time with my heartbeat.

I hover over the final key.

I finish this or I stop pretending.

I draw a breath.

I—

Something prickles at the base of my neck.

Sharp.

Sudden.

Instinctive.

Not danger in the room—danger behind it.

The hum shifts.
The air shifts.
I freeze.
Slowly—very slowly—I turn.

Chapter 34: Predator's Question

Tiberius

The hum of the Sanctum deepens as she turns—but it isn't just the room.

It's something in *me*.

A low, internal shift. An involuntary pull in my chest, like an instinct waking up after years of silence. Like the machinery in my bones reconfigures when her eyes meet mine.

I step out of the shadows, each footfall deliberate—loud enough for her to hear, quiet enough to remind her she missed them. The glass and black steel around us drink the sound and feed it back in low vibrations.

The holo-code drifting above the consoles casts shifting patterns across her face.

And for the first time, I see her clearly.

Young.

Alert.

Terrified, but hiding it with teeth.

Familiar.

Too familiar.

The recognition isn't a thought—it's a *jolt*.

A static snap under my skin.

A pull low in my ribs, like gravity deciding to anchor itself somewhere behind her sternum instead of mine.

I shouldn't feel that.

Not with an intruder.

Not with anyone.

I bury it instantly.

I let none of it show.

I keep the predator mask on as easily as breathing.

"You're a long way from the lower sectors, aren't you?"

Smooth. Controlled.

The voice I reserve for extracting truth and fear at the same time.

She stiffens, but she doesn't run.

Her chin lifts a fraction of a degree—a dare disguised as defiance.

Bold.

Or reckless.

Or predisposed to ruin.

"Funny thing," I continue, stepping closer, "the system logged two biometric anomalies tonight. One was mine. The other..."

I tilt my head, letting the pale blue holo-light hit my eyes—I want her to *feel* the scrutiny, "...doesn't belong here."

That's when it happens.

Recognition hits her too.

Not the cautious kind—the involuntary, visceral kind that slams into the nervous system first.

Her breath snags.

Her pupils narrow, then flare.

Fight-or-flight tangles with something she clearly wasn't expecting.

Good.

I'm not the only one thrown off-balance.

My gaze tracks her—but the pull beneath it is anything but.

The clearance tag.

The Undergrid scuff on her boots.

The resistance-grade stitching beneath her collar—exactly where her pulse jumps against the fabric.

Her pulse. Why did I notice her pulse?

Wrong question.

Wrong reaction.

And I can't stop analyzing her like a threat and something else entirely.

"So tell me, thief..." I let the word slip like a hand closing around a throat, testing pressure, "...who sent you to steal from my father's empire?"

She inhales sharply.

Not fear—bracing.

Heat behind it, like anger wrapped around a secret.

And she lifts her chin.

Something in my chest tightens.

Damn it.

✦ ☽⋆☾ ✦

Aly

His presence floods the chamber like cold water—but it hits my body like a *current*.

Sharp. Electric. Wrong in a way that feels dangerously right.

Fear spikes through my veins, but something else slides in beneath it—awareness.

My skin prickles.

My heartbeat stumbles.

My breath shortens in a way that has nothing to do with terror and everything to do with the man standing in front of me.

Tiberius Braxton.

Dominion's son.

The Empire's ghost.

The man who keeps the knives clean.

The man whose father executed my mother three years ago.

I should feel nothing but hatred.

I expect only hatred.

But something traitorous flickers underneath—the body recognizing danger before the mind can stop it.

I match his stare even though my knees want to give.

"No one," I say. My voice tightens, but I hold it together with sheer will. "And I am not a thief."

He stops a few paces away.

Close enough that the temperature shifts—not colder, but sharper.

Close enough that I can smell the clean bite of his uniform, the sterile metal of the Sanctum, the faint ozone tang of static from his gloves.

Close enough that I'm aware of the height difference, the proximity, the controlled stillness of him.

He studies me like a man taking me apart bolt by bolt.

But beneath the cold calculation is something else—something I shouldn't be able to see.

Recognition.

His gaze flicks down my throat, my wrists, my stance.

But it lingers just a heartbeat too long at the rise of my breath.

A fraction too long on the tension in my mouth.

He's analyzing me.

And noticing me.

A slow, dangerous smile curves across his lips.

"Not a thief," he repeats softly.

The softness is the blade.

The softness is worse than violence.

"So you break into a level-seven Empyrium archive in the dead of night for... sightseeing?"

He steps closer.

My pulse misfires.

Heat crawls up my spine.

Not attraction—no, not that—but awareness sharpened into something that borders on it, twisted by fear and fury.

"Something like that," I say.

The holo-light refracts over his face—sharp cheekbone, sharper gaze. Shadows carving the edges of his jaw. Every line of him dangerous. Beautiful in the terrible way of weapons.

"I could call the enforcers right now."

His voice lowers, pulls.

Not seducing—interrogating.

But something about the drop in tone scrapes across my nerves like an invitation I want to hate.

"Or," he leans in slightly—enough that the air between us thins, "you could tell me what you're really after. Maybe I decide it's not worth reporting."

The space between us warms.

Not physically—emotionally.

Charged.

Impossible.

For half a breath his tone softens.

Almost human.

Almost like he's speaking to me, not the intruder I'm supposed to be.

Then it seals off.

Cold. Unreachable.

"But lie to me again," he says, straightening, the steel sliding back into place, "and you'll wish I'd handed you to them instead."

He waits.

Silent.

Still.

Predator.

Watching every flicker of my face.

Watching to see if I flinch.

Watching to see if I break.

And for the first time, beneath the terror, beneath the grief, beneath the mission—

I feel something I don't want to name.

A pull. A spark. A wrongness that feels like inevitability.

Because this isn't menace for show.

This is the only language he's ever been allowed to speak.

And somehow, some terrible, instinctive part of me recognizes it.

Recognizes *him*.

Even if it shouldn't.

Even if I don't want it to.

Even if it's going to ruin everything.

Tiberius

She doesn't answer right away.

She doesn't flinch the way most do when I strip the room to silence.

Instead, she holds my stare—jaw tight, pulse visible at her throat, fear warring with something fiercer underneath.

Something that hits me again, harder this time.

Recognition.

Pull.

Spark.

No.

Not spark.

Not that.

I lock the thought down before it forms fully.

Before it can breathe.

But my body betrays me for a single, treacherous second—

a heat low in my chest, a magnetic tilt of instinct that has no place here, no explanation, no permission.

It feels like stepping toward a memory I don't have.

Like I've been here before.

Faced her before.

Chosen something before.

Impossible.

Unacceptable.

I shove it down so fast it feels like cauterizing a wound.

"Well?" I say.

My voice stays level, but something inside me is not.

The Sanctum hums around us.

Her breath catches.

The air between us sharpens, stretches thin.

This should feel simple.

Routine.

A threat and an intruder.

A problem and a solution.

It doesn't.

And I hate that I don't know why.

For a heartbeat—one I ignore as soon as it hits—I feel her fear, her defiance, that spark inside her like it's echoing down a line between us that shouldn't exist.

A line that I will sever.

Must sever.

Because whatever this is—this flicker of familiarity, this wrong gravity, this recognition without memory—

...it is a threat.

To my mission.

To my control.

To the version of myself Dominion forged.

So I bury it.

Deep.

Where he'll never see it.

Where *I* won't.

But the echo stays.

Unwanted.

Unshakable.
There in the quiet, in the space between her lifted chin and my held breath.
A pull I refuse to name.
A pull I will never admit exists.

Chapter 35: Names Like Fire

Tiberius

She turns.

And the moment she does, something shifts—not in the vault, not in the tech, but in *me.*

Like gravity hiccups.

Like a pressure change inside my chest collapses inward.

Like recognition slams into instinct, bypassing thought.

And for one impossible heartbeat, the whole world pares down to two things:

Her eyes—indigo blue, familiar and deadly—and the truth she hasn't spoken yet.

She shouldn't feel familiar.

But she does.

In a way that's too sharp to be coincidence, too immediate to be memory.

There's no hesitation in the way she holds my gaze.

Only the tremble in her hands gives her away—and even that tremble isn't fear.

It's will.

Defiance stretched to razor-thin steel.

A pressure gathers behind my ribs, sharp and unfamiliar, a recognition I keep trying to deny but can't fully extinguish.

Not after the moment she lifted her chin at me like she'd been waiting her entire life to defy someone like me.

She takes a long breath, gathering herself.

Her voice wavers but doesn't break.

"I'm not lying."

There's a steadiness under the shake—an iron buried under all that aching grief.

The kind you only hear from people who've already survived more than the Empire ever planned for them.

And something in my bones reacts.

A flicker.

A resonance.

Something that feels like an old echo waking up, answering a sound I didn't know I'd been waiting to hear.

My throat tightens before I catch it.

Before I crush it.

She exhales once, long and controlled.

"I'm here for my mother's records."

The hum of the vault holds still—like the room itself is listening.

"I want to delete them," she says.

"Her last orders to me before she... died."

She breaks on the last word.

A fracture.

A wound.

The sound hits me like a hit to the sternum—clean, painful, human.

A weakness I can't afford to feel.

A pull I refuse to acknowledge.

Delete them.

A strike-match dragged across dry nerves.

Too bold.

Too reckless.

Too... human.

"Ambition," I murmur, the sound soft, almost amused.

"Or a funeral pyre?"

She startles at my tone—not because it's cruel, but because it isn't.

I don't move yet.

I watch her instead.

How her pulse stutters.

How her shoulders square anyway.

How she carries grief like armor instead of chains.

How her presence pulls at something inside me I'm not prepared to name.

"You speak of orders from the dead like excuses for arson."

I step closer, slow and deliberate—close enough that the heat from my suit brushes her jacket.

Close enough that her breath stutters again.

Close enough that the gravity between us makes the air feel thick.

She swallows.

Her pulse jumps.

And when I step closer—

—heat snaps between us.

Not physical heat.

Not attraction.

Something deeper.

Heavier.

Like the space between our bodies compresses,

recognizes itself,

tightens with something older than logic.

I lean one hand on the console beside her, close enough that my breath stirs the collar of her jacket.

Close enough that I feel the force of her pulse against the air.

Close enough that every sense sharpens to her.

If I were anyone else,

I'd step back.

If I were the version of myself Dominion built,

I wouldn't have stepped forward to begin with.

"Do you know what happens to those who try to erase empire history? We don't just strip names. We strip futures."

The words come out flat—ledger lines, not threats.

The way I was trained to speak.

The way he molded me.

I plant one gloved hand against the console, leaning into her space just enough to test her spine—and test the pull that keeps snapping between us when I get too close.

"Tell me the name of your mother. If you lie, I'll find the enforcers and personally watch them pull what's left of you apart—metaphorically speaking."

The silence tightens around us.

A blade.

A breath.

A test neither of us wants to be the first to lose.

I pause.

Let it bite.

Let it settle deep into her bones.

"If you tell the truth," I add, voice low, almost intimate, "I'll decide if you're useful."

Even as something under my skin hums with a strange, quiet pressure—an instinct pulling toward her as fiercely as duty pulls away.

Her breath shivers, but her chin lifts.

Good.

Fight me.

Don't collapse.

The vault lights flicker.

Something inside me responds to that fight—a flicker of heat I crush the second it sparks.

"Deleting records is messy," I add, quieter, almost clinical.

"Loud. If you really want to end a legacy, there are cleaner ways."

The holo-screen flickers.

I glance at it—and a fragment of the manifest she'd pulled up earlier spills across the glass:

L. Carmichael—Transfer 42-B—Executed

A name like a wound.

My father's ledger.

His cruelty written in cold ink.

No.

It can't be.

Not possible.

Not fate's twisted sense of humor.

I level my gaze at her again.

"Why the Braxton's wanted her gone.

Give me the truth and—maybe—I'll think about saving you from my father's enforcers."

There's an edge in my voice I didn't put there.

Too sharp.

Too personal.

Too close to something I don't want to feel.

I step back half a breath, folding my hands.

A choice disguised as a threat.

A threat disguised as a mercy.

Either way, the gravity between us doesn't fade.

It sharpens.

✦ ☽★☾ ✦

Aly

He steps closer—and the air between us tightens like wire.

Heat radiates off him,

but not warmth.

Something more volatile.

Awareness.

Pressure.

A gravity that shouldn't exist.

He leans over me, hand braced on the console.

His shoulder blocks the holo-light, casting us both in shadow.

I shouldn't notice the line of his jaw at this distance.

I shouldn't feel the shape of his breath against my cheek.

I shouldn't feel... anything.

I huff out a small laugh.

Not because this is funny,

but because everything is so impossible it loops back into it.

The thought *is* funny—because telling **him** the truth will damn me anyway.

"If I told you without lying," I say, heart hammering harder the closer he stands, "you'd hand me over anyway."

His smile is slow—

the kind that forms like frost,

measured and quiet and dangerous.

Except... there's something warmer underneath, flickering too quickly to pin down.

He steps closer again, until I can see the tiny scar along his jaw.

Proof he's been somewhere bloody.

Somewhere real.

Somewhere human.

"Maybe I would," he says, voice low enough the holo-glow doesn't quite catch it. "Maybe I'd hand you to the enforcers and watch the city applaud."

The words should terrify me.

They don't.

Because something in him softens a breath before it shutters.

Because something in me recognizes the fracture where the softness leaks through.

"Or maybe I'd keep you here and use you until you're so useful you stop being a liability."

The words slide over me cold, but his tone glances warm for half a beat—softening before he suffocates it again.

Heat spikes in my chest.

Not attraction.

Not exactly.

Recognition.

Of grief.

Of pain.

Of someone who knows what it is to bury a name.

He leans closer again.

Close enough our breaths tangle.

"Which do you prefer? Martyr or asset?"

He taps the console.

The manifest ripples again.

My mother's name flickers like a ghost.

Executed.

The cold in my chest ignites.

Becomes something sharp enough to breathe.

The pain inside me burns hotter.

Brighter.

Sharper.

And when he looks at me—

really looks at me—

something in his eyes cracks wide open.

Almost like he recognizes me too.

Like he feels the same wrong pull that keeps striking between us.

Tiberius's rain-forest green eyes flick to mine.

Waiting.

Measuring.

Pulling at something he doesn't want to acknowledge.

"Tell me why the Braxton's wanted her gone," he repeats.

A jagged thing wrapped in silk.

"One truth," he says.

"One choice."

Damned if I do.

Damned if I don't.

But I've come too far in truth to choke on it now.

And god—

I'm tired.

Tired of the war.

Tired of the weight.

Tired of being the shadow of someone else's legend.

Tired of carrying a name like a battlefield.

I take a breath.

A deep one.

"I'm Alysa Carmichael," I say. The name falls from my lips like ash from a dying star.

"Lara Carmichael *was* my mother."

For one impossible second—

it feels like a weight lifts off my shoulders.

Tiberius's face changes.

Not flinching.

Not recoiling.

Recognition.

Like his soul flinches first, before his body can hide it.

"Before she was captured," I continue, "she gave me orders. To destroy her file if she died."

I step closer—

not threatening,

not pleading—

just *meeting him as an equal* for the first time.

"And I am the Ash Commander.

The reason the rebellion didn't collapse after her death.

The reason it's still going."

Shock hits him so visibly it steals the air between us.

His breath stutters.

He steps back—not because he wants distance, but because he doesn't know what to do with the gravity between us.

The truth spills out of me faster than I can stop it—

raw, unguarded, desperate—

and it feels so good to finally speak it out loud and *to him* of all people.

"And..."

my voice softens, cracking at the edges,

"I never wanted it."

The truth I've carried alone since the moment my mother fell.

Tiberius

Everything freezes.

The hum.

The air.

My pulse.

Alysa Carmichael.

A name like fire.

A name I was never supposed to hear from her mouth.

The girl from the warehouse.

The ghost from the arena.

The intruder in this Sanctum.

The Ash Commander of the rebellion.

And the last words Lara Carmichael whispered as she died—

the ones I heard,

the ones that haunt me every time I close my eyes—

"The rebellion will not die with me."

My breath stutters.

The ledger isn't numbers anymore.

It's human.

It's her.

Standing in front of me.

Looking at me without fear.

Without apology.

Without anything but truth.

The mask—the one I've worn since I was old enough to follow orders—cracks.

And the part of me that should feel nothing—

the part Dominion hammered into steel—

flares with something I cannot name.

Something dangerous.

Something undeniable.

Something like the beginning of resonance.

My mask fractures more.

Not enough for her to see—

but enough for me to feel.

Enough to know I will never look at this girl the same way again.

Enough to know this moment just rewrote every line of my future.

Enough to know—

Nothing about this girl is coincidence.

Nothing about this moment is routine.

And nothing about the way she looks at me

will let me walk out of this vault unchanged.

Alysa Carmichael isn't just an enemy.

She is a fault line in the world I was raised to uphold.

And I'm already standing on it.

Chapter 36: The Warehouse, Remembered

Tiberius

Alysa Carmichael.

The true ghost of the Empire.

The woman standing in my father's sanctum.

The girl whose name cracked something open in my chest.

In the corner of the holo-display, a red countdown flickers to life:

PURGE DELAY: 04:00

Fuck.

Four minutes.

I drag my gaze from the timer back to her.

I should call this in.

I don't.

Instead, I hear myself say,

"*You want me to believe you, then prove it.*"

My hand lifts—gloved fingers hovering over the console—not to trigger the purge, but to steady myself.

It's ridiculous that she affects me enough to need steadying.

But the gravity between us is wrong.

Too familiar.

Too real.

"Tell me one thing only the real leader of the rebellion would know," I say. "Something small. Verifiable. A phrase. A place. A name."

I let the threat sharpen my tone, but my voice dips lower than intended.

Danger, closeness, and something under the surface I refuse to name.

"If it's true, I don't hand you to the enforcers tonight. If it's false—"

I don't need to finish.

The red strobe paints the glass and her face in alternating pulses—

03:52

03:51

Her throat bobs.

She doesn't look away.

"My title is important," she says quietly. "Whether *I'm* important is...

debatable. But if you insist, then very well."

She steps closer.

Not a timid step.

A deliberate one.

A step that pulls the air tight between us—thin, heated, aware.

Close enough that I feel her breath when she leans in.

"I know who *you are*," she whispers against my ear.

Her breath ghosts along my jaw—soft, warm.

It shouldn't affect me.

It does.

No reverence.

No fear.

She steps back, eyes flicking to the holo-screens, then resting on my face with... empathy. Of all things.

It hits me like a blow.

"I know you don't want anyone to know who you are. Or your father doesn't, anyway." Her voice stays soft.

Steady.

Dangerously perceptive.

"You are the Empire's ghost, Tiberius Braxton."

Something in my chest locks.

I go still.

Stillness is my tell.

I've trained an empire not to see it.

She does.

"Careful," I say. It should be a warning.

It sounds... tired.

"You don't know what you've stepped into."

My gaze flicks to the countdown—

03:27

Then back to her.

"If my father finds out you've even *guessed—*"

The sentence fractures in my throat.

For the first time, I can't tell if I'm warning her or myself.

"You should've lied, Alysa," I murmur. "You should've run when you saw my face."

She doesn't flinch. Her expression stays the same.

"Do you know how I knew who you were?" she asks.

Something hot coils low in my chest—anticipation, dread, recognition.

I half-smile.

It feels wrong—sharp, defensive, cracking at the edges.

"Prove it then," I say.

"Prove that you know who I am."

I keep my eyes on the red glow of the purge clock—

03:12

"Most people find out the usual way," I add.

"Rumor. A leaked report. A mistake in the data stream."

Then I look at her fully.

"But you said it like you'd seen it for yourself. So? How did you know?"

The question hangs between us—bare, soft, and too honest.

The siren hums louder.

03:02

She takes a breath.

And when she speaks, it isn't a weapon.

It's memory.

✦ ☽⋆☾ ✦

Aly

The memory came sharp and painful just like the night it happened.

"Being invisible growing up," I say, "you see things. Hear things."

The hum of the cooling stacks rises in my ears.

Anything to drown out the timer bleeding red light across the console.

"I've known who you were for a long time."

His eyes tighten—microscopically, but enough.

A tell he never meant to give me.

"I was about sixteen the first time I saw you," I say. "It was raining."

The Sanctum smells like cold metal and recycled air—

but in my mind, it's wet stone, ozone, and bodies that didn't get to breathe again.

"I was on a mission," I say. "the warehouse on Fort Worth Ave. I was the only one who came back from that warehouse alive."

The siren crackles louder.

02:41

My pulse spikes: I know what that count down means, and it's not good.

"I stopped in a tavern to drown out the memory of watching my friends die."

My voice wavers. Once. "Some men were talking about the ruler's son. One said, '*He should be here any second.*'"

I meet his eyes.

"And then you stepped through the doors."

His jaw ticks.

Barely.

But the impact is sharp.

"One of them said, *'And the ghost appears.'* And that was when I put it together. The ruler's son. The ghost of the Empyrium. One and the same."

I swallow.

"You killed my whole squad," I say softly. "And... somehow missed the most important one."

His breath catches.

Sharp. Raw.

Like I struck something buried too deep to name.

"You've known who I was for years and kept your mouth shut," he says. "That tells me either you're very smart... or you're tired of playing by anyone's rules but your own."

He steps toward the console—toward me.

Heat passes between us.

Quiet, electric.

Wrong.

"Which is it?"

"Whether it was by accident or on purpose," I say, "you didn't kill me that night. I owed you that much. I'm not playing by any rules."

I don't step back.

"That night changed me in more ways than I can count."

His eyes flick over me—

not as an intruder,

not as a threat,

but as someone he's seeing again for the first time.

"Besides," I add, breath unsteady, "you looked tired of it all then. Just like you do now."

The memory hangs between us—

rain, fire, steam lifting off bodies,

a boy with dead eyes watching a street burn.

"I should have seen a monster," I whisper. "I didn't. I saw someone who'd already burned with the buildings."

The purge clock drops:

02:09

The siren hum is a held scream vibrating inside my bones.

He looks at me like he's never been seen before.

Tiberius

"Fort Worth Ave," I say. The name tastes like smoke. The memory hit worse.

"That was a long night."

Too long.

Too loud.

Too much blood.

"You shouldn't have been anywhere near that district," I say.

"No one came out of that mission whole."

Guilt tightens my shoulders before I can hide it.

The feeling is foreign.

Unwanted.

Undeniable.

She doesn't look away.

"I gave the order that night," I say.

The words hollow themselves out as they leave me.

"I watched the drones light the street and told myself it was efficient."

The first explosion echoes in my ribs—

flash, heat, screams swallowed by steam.

"If you're still here after hearing that," I say quietly, "then you understand something most don't."

"It took a year before I could stand the sound of rain again."

My voice isn't steady.

Neither is the ground under us.

I look at her.

"The Empire runs on ghosts. People we erase so it keeps standing."

Her mother.

Her squad.

Me.

The siren ticks:

01:31

"If you think you owed me something for missing you..."

I shake my head.

"Consider it settled. No one should owe anyone for surviving."

I drag in a breath that sticks in my chest.

"You said that night changed you," I say. "Good. Change is the only thing that keeps us from turning into the machines that built this place."

I step closer.

Not to intimidate.

Not to control.

But because something in me can't stand the distance between us anymore.

"You saw me then," I say. "Not a monster. A tired boy."

The admission lands between us—fragile, painful, real.

"So here we are," I add.

"The girl who survived the kill order. And the ghost of the empire that gave it."

My voice drops.

"If you want to erase a legacy..." I nod toward the console. Toward myself. "So do I."

I meet her eyes.

Not as an interrogator.

Not as Dominion's son.

As the boy who walked into that tavern dripping rain and regret.

"What do you want, Alysa?" I say. "Not what your mother wanted. Not the rebellion. ***You.***"

The purge clock hits:

01:00

✦ ☽⋆☾ ✦

Aly

The question hits harder than any explosion.

Harder than the siren.

Harder than the warehouse.

No one has ever asked me that.

My throat feels too tight.

"It doesn't matter what I want," I whisper. "We're both bound to what we inherited. Would it even matter?"

That's the script I know.

That's the cage I live in.

But he studies me—

blue light slicing across his face—

and he looks like he's asking the question for himself too.

"That's the problem," he says softly. "We spend so long pretending what we inherited *is* what we are."

His jaw tightens.

Truth looks wrong on him—

too honest, too human.

"My father calls that loyalty," he says.

"I call it a cage."

00:42

"It does matter what you want, Alysa," he says.

"It's the only way to survive people like him. If you stop wanting anything... they've already won."

My chest tightens.

My eyes burn.

No one has ever said that to me.

Not Kai.

Not Axel.

Not Vivian.

Not even my mother.

The siren's hum presses against my ribs like a second heartbeat.

I don't have to think about it. I know exactly what I want—and it escapes before I can stop it.

"I want to be free," I breathe.

The words fall out of me like a confession.

Not victory.

Not vengeance.

Freedom.

Freedom from expectation.

Freedom from legacy.

Freedom from the blood on my hands and the weight in my bones.

The truth burns on the way out.

I swallow hard.

Then a thought hits me.

"What do *you* want, Tiberius?" I ask.

If I'm bleeding the truth, so is he.

He doesn't answer right away.

The hum, the siren, the faint static from his gloves—

all of it wraps around us like a current.

Finally he says,

"Freedom."

His voice breaks on it.

Quiet.

Honest.

Unscripted.

"I was born in a cage made of gold, protocol, and obedience. Everyone says I have power, but every command, every breath is scripted."

He looks at me.

Really looks.

"I want out."

The purge clock blinks:

00:20

We stand there in the empire's heart—

the girl who survived his fire,

the boy who gave the order—

And for the first time,

we see each other.

Not monster.

Not ghost.

Just two people who are very, very tired of cages.
The siren climbs a note.
Time is almost up.

Chapter 37: Erasure

Tiberius

00:20

Twenty seconds before the purge protocol triggers.

Twenty seconds before the vault floods with drones, scanners, and fire.

Twenty seconds to decide what kind of man I am.

Alysa stands in front of me, shoulders locked tight, defiance burning through the fear like a secondary pulse.

She should look small in this room—in this empire.

She doesn't.

"If I wanted freedom," I say, "I'd have to burn everything he built. Including myself."

For the first time, the truth sits openly between us.

Not hidden under rank.

Not buried under obedience.

Just there—bare, trembling, real.

The exhale that leaves me isn't a laugh. Not really.

More like something breaking open that's been sealed for years.

"Maybe that's why you're still breathing, Alysa Carmichael," I say quietly. "Because for the first time in a long time... someone in this empire said what I've been trying not to think."

I step closer—not as a threat, not as a captor—just near enough that honesty feels possible.

Near enough that the wrong gravity between us tightens, familiar in a way that terrifies me.

"You want to be free," I murmur.

"And I want to know what that feels like."

00:17. 00:16

"The question is..." I meet her eyes head-on, "can two people bound by the same chains free each other—or just tighten them?"

She holds my gaze.

And for a heartbeat, everything in the room feels too loud—

the hum, the siren, the air between us stretching thin.

I wait for truth—not obedience.

✦ ☽⋆☾ ✦

Aly

Heat coils up my spine—anger, fear, something stranger.

"I have no intention of tightening them," I snap. "I've already suffocated enough. I don't want this anymore."

My eyes flick to the corridor—no exit.

No windows.

Trapped.

Then back to him.

"We want the same thing, right?" I whisper. "Then maybe we can help each other."

My breath is fast, but steady—steady because he's steady, and I hate that.

Or maybe I need it.

"I'm putting my life in your hands," I say—

probably the most insane sentence I've ever spoken.

"You can either save me... or turn me in."

The truth vibrates between us like an exposed wire.

✦ ☽⋆☾ ✦

Tiberius

For once, I don't hide the decision forming inside me.

Something in me sharpens—not into cruelty, but clarity.

She's not bargaining with me.

She's giving me the choice the Empire never did.

I inhale slowly, turn toward the console, and lift my hand.

00:13. 00:12

One command:

Cameras—**off**.

Another:

Patrol feed—**neutralized**.

Third:

Purge protocol—**delayed**.

The red warning lights sputter, flicker—

and die.

The hum of drones fades into static.

The vault stills.

The silence that replaces the siren is louder than the alarm ever was.

"Then we start here," I say.

Now I step to her—not as predator, not as soldier.

As someone who, for the first time in years, has made a choice that is *mine.*

Alysa looks at me like she's not sure whether to breathe or run—

and something in me mirrors the feeling.

"You walk out of this vault alive," I tell her, "and nobody remembers you were here."

I don't step toward her as a captor.

I step toward her as someone choosing.

My voice drops lower—soft, dangerous in its honesty.

"I can keep the empire's eyes off you for a while. Long enough for us to decide what freedom looks like when it's not just a word."

I glance back at the console—her mother's redacted file still glowing like a scar.

"You don't owe me trust," I admit. "But if you stay, you'll need to act like you do."

She pauses just for a moment, then says, "I can do that."

Then, softer than I intend:

"I promise I'll erase your mother's file myself. Completely."

Her breath catches.

"Walk beside me," I tell her. "Don't run."

Her eyes are still on me.

"And Alysa..."

Her name hits my tongue like something sharp and fragile.

"...don't make me regret giving you a choice."

✦ ☽⋆☾ ✦

Aly

I almost laugh—because pretending trust is nothing new.

Not because of his offer—

because pretending trust has been my entire life.

But trusting him...

that feels different.

I nod once.

And for the first time, he looks like he believes me.

Not the Ash Commander.

Not the rebel's daughter.

Just... me.

Tiberius

I give her one short nod—an oath without words.

The vault door unseals with a soft hiss—

quiet enough not to alert the next patrol, loud enough to sound like the start of something irreversible.

"Stay close," I murmur.

We step out of the Sanctum together.

And as the door slides shut behind us, I say the truth aloud for the first time:

"If you're staying in this game, Alysa," I tell her. "You need to understand something. Lies aren't meant to hide truth. They're meant to *buy time* for it.

The door seals.

The purge clock resets.

The lights return to Empyrium white.

But nothing in me resets.

And for the first time,

I'm not the perfect son walking out of this room.

I'm the man who chose her.

Chapter 38: The First Truce

Aly

The corridor outside the vault feels colder than the Sanctum—narrow, bright, lined with mirrored panels that throw our reflections back at us like ghosts walking beside ghosts.

Tiberius moves first.

Not fast.

Just with the kind of quiet authority that suggests the walls were built to part for him.

"For now," he murmurs, voice low and crisp, "you're a tech contractor. I'll update the entry logs before we reach the lift. Keep your head down. Don't meet anyone's eyes. And if someone speaks to you—let me answer."

It's a command.

But it's thinner now—less absolute, more careful.

Like he's newly aware of every crack in his tone, every place where control slid between his fingers tonight.

I nod once and fall into step beside him.

The mirrored walls catch our shapes:

he walks like a contained storm,

I walk like someone who's spent years learning to be invisible.

Together... we almost look like we belong here.

Halfway down the corridor, he glances sideways without turning his head.

"You said you can pretend trust," he says. "Keep pretending."

His voice dips—quieter, rawer, dangerously close to honest.

"It might keep you alive long enough for both of us to figure out whether we're actually on the same side."

A smirk slips out of me—small, involuntary.

And through the mirrored panel, I catch him watching me.

Not a quick look.

A slow, deliberate drag of attention—

the kind that makes my pulse miss the next beat.

He doesn't turn.

He just studies me through the glass, like he can map every shift in my breath without risking looking directly.

"Oh, the sweet irony," I mutter under my breath.

His mouth twitches.

Not a smile—he's too cautious for that.

But the ghost of it curves his mouth in a way that sends heat crawling up my throat.

"Irony is the Empire's favorite joke," he says dryly. "It keeps us all believing we have choices."

We reach the lift core.

The doors slide open with a soft hiss—warm air brushing my face like a warning.

Inside, the lift is all black steel and blue-gold light, humming faintly as if it knows exactly how dangerous this moment is.

He enters first.

Waits.

I follow.

The doors seal, and neon light from the city spills upward through the glass shaft—the underground giving way to the surface in ribbons of harsh blue and hot gold.

Tiberius's gaze shifts—

not to me,

but to my reflection in the glass.

That sideways intimacy again.

Safer than direct eye contact.

More dangerous because it allows him to look longer.

"You're about to walk into the heart of everything your mother fought against," he says softly.

"Stay close, listen, and don't speak until we're clear."

Then, almost too low to catch:

"If we're very careful, Alysa Carmichael... we might just survive long enough to find out what freedom feels like."

Freedom.

The word pulses—

low, hot, unsettling.

Another smirk tugs at my mouth—quieter this time.

Uncontrolled.

Real.

The kind my generals hated.

The kind that feels like choosing myself.

Tiberius notices.

Of course he does.

"Keep that smirk when we pass the guards," he murmurs.

"Confidence is harder to trace than fear."

His voice wraps around the last word, warm and sharp at the same time.

The lift slows—gliding toward the public access tier.

The hum shifts into a tighter, higher pitch, like even the machinery senses the lie we're stepping into.

Almost time.

My heart hits once—too loud, too fast.

My heart thuds once, hard enough that I pray the lift walls won't echo it back.

Before the doors open, I turn my jacket inside out—

hiding the stitched rank, hiding her name.

The fabric is old, softened by years, but I'm not stepping into the Empire's spotlight wearing a target.

Tiberius's brows lift.

Not in disapproval—

in something sharper, warmer, almost startled.

A flicker of heat-tinged attention.

A heartbeat of appraisal.

Approval... and something else behind it, something he reins in the second it sparks.

Then—he moves.

Not abruptly.

Just a shift of weight, a step closer, close enough that the warm exhale of his breath brushes my cheek as he reaches toward my collar.

"Hold still," he murmurs.

His fingers brush the edge of the jacket—straightening a fold that didn't need straightening.

An excuse.

A pretext.

A deliberate choice to close the last inches between us.

My breath hitches—sharp, involuntary.

Heat flares low in my ribs, a pulse I can't control fast enough.

His hand pauses for half a second—feeling the reaction he wasn't supposed to get.

His gaze drops, just once, to my mouth in the reflection.

Then he shuts the moment down with a quiet inhale, as if locking the impulse behind his ribs.

"There," he says softly.

"Now you look like you belong here."

He steps back exactly as the lift doors glide open—

as if he timed the distance, the closeness, the heat—

down to the second.

I take a breath and clear my throat,

"Call me Alysa Tobias. It's what I go by rather than Carmichael. Safer."

Tiberius

The name hits like a cipher handed to me in the dark—

a secret pressed into my palm warm from her voice.

"Alysa Tobias," I repeat softly.

Testing the shape of it.

Letting it settle on my tongue in a way it shouldn't.

"It rolls off the tongue better than 'traitor's daughter.'"

It should sting.

But there's no venom left in me.

Only irony... and something heated enough that I have to look at her reflection instead of her actual face.

I lean in—

not touching her, just close enough that the air lifts between us,

close enough that she feels it.

Her breath catches—

so subtle most people wouldn't notice.

I do.

"Names are currency here," I tell her.

"Protect yours."
I pause a moment.
"I'll protect the rest."
The lift doors slide open.
Cold neon light spills across both our reflections—
two figures aligned by necessity,
not touching,
but no longer at odds.
The first truce. And the first step into the lie that might save us both.

Chapter 39: The Outer Exchange

Aly

The neon tier hits like a slap of cold light and noise.

Drizzle misting down from the overhead conduits.

Crowds weaving in tight, restless patterns.

Drone lights sweeping surveillance arcs that skim across every face like a blade deciding who to cut.

For a moment, instinct spikes sharp and primal.

Run.

But Tiberius steps forward instead—

calm, composed, adjusting his cuffs like he could straighten the entire Empire with one precise gesture.

"We'll start at the outer exchange," he says.

Tone clipped, but lower than before.

Controlled, but not cold.

Measured in the way someone sounds when a night has already cracked something inside them.

"You'll shadow me while I handle a shipment authorization. It gives us time to build a story."

He moves before I can answer—

expecting me to follow.

So I do.

Not because I trust him.

Not yet.

But because the path he cuts through the chaos feels... precise.

Deliberate.

Safe, in the most dangerous possible way.

And for the first time—

it feels like we are stepping into a war

side by side.

The city swallows us whole.

One of the Empire's most dangerous men,

and the rebellion's hidden heir,

walking in sync like we're not a contradiction sharp enough to split the neon night open.

He threads us through the outer market with practiced ease.

People shift around him instantly—

not out of fear,

but in that quiet, instinctive way citizens move for someone who is woven into the Empire's architecture.

He walks like someone who knows how the city breathes—

when scanners blink,

when guards exhale,

where the blind spots live.

"Lies aren't to hide truth," he murmurs, almost to himself.

"They buy time for it."

I roll my eyes but match his pace.

Buying time is what I'm good at.

Lying?

Harder.

At least to him. For some strange reason... I can't.

Not like I do with everyone else.

I can't explain why.

"Very well, Tiberius," I mutter, smirking before I can stop myself.

A flicker of humor ghosts across his mouth.

Quick.

Contained.

Dangerously unguarded.

We reach the checkpoint.

Metal gates.

Armed inspectors.

ID scanners humming with the monotone heartbeat of the Empire.

A hawk-faced woman steps forward.

"Shipment authorization, Lord Braxton."

Tiberius flicks his wrist.

A bloom of code spreads across her tablet—

not forged.

Not faked.

Redirected, like the system itself wants to obey him.

"Bringing on an analyst to audit ledger discrepancies," he says, bored.

"She's new. I'll need expedited processing."

The inspector's gaze snaps to me—

a cold, slicing second.

"Name?"

Tiberius answers before I breathe.

"Alysa Tobias. Contract appointment."

Green light.

Hiss of the gates.

We're through.

My knees stay steady.

Barely.

The city swallows us again—

neon haze, static, ozone.

Tiberius hands me a datapad.

Blank.

Clean.

Perfectly plausible.

"Play the part," he murmurs.

Voice lower.

Rougher.

Carrying something that wasn't there hours ago.

"Scan receipts. Nod. Let me answer questions. You do exactly what I say and no one dies tonight."

His thumb brushes the datapad—

an unconscious rhythm.

A repeated touch that lands under my skin like a pulse I shouldn't feel.

"You know why you couldn't lie to me?" he murmurs.

I say nothing.

He does.

"Because you're not used to men who don't want to see you burn."

A pause.

"That's not mercy, Alysa. That's interest."

No threat.

No softness.

Just truth.

"Dangerous kind of interest," he adds.

Heat licks the back of my neck.

Not fear.

Something I don't want to name.

We move again—

flowing around a broker with a trolley of sealed cases.

"Keep your smirk," he murmurs. "It suits you."

A breath catches in my throat—

pure reflex.

"Freedom doesn't look like fireworks," he adds.

"It looks like folding a paper small enough to hide in your pocket. One careful choice at a time."

His words land heavier than they should.

"And how would *you* know what freedom looks like?" I ask.

"I've only known men who want to see me burn. What makes you different?"

He looks at me.

Not harsh.

Not soft.

Just... direct.

He doesn't speak immediately.

The silence between us vibrates like a line pulled taut.

Finally:

"I don't. Not really."

He doesn't look away.

"Freedom is a rumor people like me hear in the dark. My father calls it chaos. My advisers call it treason."

He exhales.

Short.

Bitter.

"I call it... a possibility I haven't learned how to live with yet."

He slows—

just enough that our shoulders almost brush.

"You asked what makes me different," he says softly.

His voice drops even lower.

"I was raised to burn people who disobey."

He pauses.

"And I learned to hate the smell of it."

Something inside me stutters.

Not fear.

Recognition.

He looks at me then—

fully, quietly—

as if the neon is painting truth over the both of us.

"You don't have to trust that," he says.

"Just use it."

Another pause.

"But if you stay with me... understand this—what we're doing isn't rebellion anymore. It's survival."

He steps away, back into the flow.

"This way, Alysa," he murmurs, voice low, almost warm.

"Let's see if we can make freedom look like an ordinary day."

Something in my chest loosens.

Dangerous.

Impossible.

"Oh, don't tempt a girl," I say lightly—

but inside...

everything feels like it's shifting.

Because he's not looking at me like a ghost.

Not like a weapon.

Not like a threat.

And somehow—

that is far more unsettling than fear.

Tiberius

I lead her into the audit wing—

a glass hall suspended above the exchange floor,

its observation balcony overlooking a swarm of traders, drones, and inspectors below.

A place built for oversight.

Control.

Power pressed into architecture.

A place where I've never stood beside anyone.

Never let anyone stand beside *me.*

Alysa steps to the glass railing—

cautious, sharp-eyed, jacket turned inside out, breathing like she's memorizing every exit.

She doesn't know how the light hits her here.

How the neon currents paint themselves across her face like war paint.

How the city's heartbeat echoes in the space between us.

I tell myself I'm watching for cracks in her cover.

But the truth lands anyway—quiet, unwanted, undeniable.

There is something wrong in the way she pulls my focus.

Something familiar in the unfamiliar.

Something like recognition.

Something like resonance.

And god help me—

I step closer.

Part V

The Spark and the Silence

*"Some connections don't ignite with touch—
they spark in the silence, in the breath between names.
And what frightened me wasn't the spark...
but how deeply it took root."
—the boy made of obedience and the girl made of ash,
reflecting each other before they ever met*

Chapter 40: Glass and Ghosts

Tiberius

The observation balcony is quiet at this hour—

quiet in the way only engineered stillness can be.

Wind hums through the rail vents.

Neon haze drifts upward from the lower tiers like the city is bleeding light instead of smoke.

Glass walls frame the skyline.

Cold. Perfect. Controllable.

I guide Alysa toward the railing, careful to keep my hands to myself but close enough that any onlooker would assume she answers to me.

She needs the cover.

So do I.

It's strange seeing her here.

Stranger seeing her in this light.

In the Data Vault she was shadow—sharp, dangerous, unyielding.

Up here, the neon outlines her edges, softens nothing, reveals everything.

For a heartbeat—

one—

something in me hesitates.

Alysa takes a step—

a small shift, but enough to close the distance between us.

She goes to move past me toward the interior hall—

and her hand brushes mine.

Not a bump.

Not a graze.

A full, warm, intentional-by-accident slide of skin against skin.

Heat snaps up my arm like a struck wire.

Her breath catches.

So does mine.

We both freeze.

One second.

Two.

Three.

Her fingers twitch—like she didn't mean to touch me, but didn't hate the contact either.

I swallow—too hard, too slow—

and pull my hand back half an inch.

Not enough to sever the moment.

Just enough to survive it.

Then:

Boots click behind us.

A security officer approaches, visor angled, posture alert. She slows when she sees Alysa.

Too slow.

A hot, unwelcome spike cracks through my ribs.

Not fear.

Something closer to anger.

"Lord Braxton," the officer says, tapping her visor to expand a scan overlay.

"We flagged an irregularity earlier. Facial-match ghost signature. Origin: Level Seven."

Alysa's breath stutters—quiet, but not quiet enough.

The officer tilts her head toward Alysa.

"Your contractor looks—"

I move between them before she finishes.

Smooth. Precise. Final.

"Officer."

My voice is a blade in a sheath.

"She's part of my audit team."

The officer hesitates.

"Sir, protocol requires—"

"You will not scan her."

Not a command.

A warning.

Her visor flicks toward Alysa again—assessing, calculating.

Something cracks hot and violent in my chest.

Not fear.

Something older.

Something I have no name for.

Something that surges faster than thought:

If you touch her, you do not walk away.

The instinct is so sudden I almost flinch.

Not at her.

At myself.

I cage the reaction immediately—jaw locking, breath cutting thin—before the feeling can sharpen into something I can't take back.

I strangle the thought before it becomes something else.

"Do you know," I say quietly, leaning in so my badge pings her visor, "what happens to personnel who imply I can't control my own team?"

She pales beneath the glass.

"No, sir."

"Then walk away."

She salutes sharply and leaves, steps quicker than before.

When the echo fades, Alysa breathes out—shallow, shaky.

"Was that... necessary?" she whispers.

I turn toward her—

toward the reflection of her in the glass,

her pulse ticking faster at her throat,

the tremor she thinks she hid.

"That wasn't for show," I say.

"She looked at you too long."

Alysa arches a brow.

"And that bothered you?"

"Yes."

The word escapes before I can drag it back.

Too fast.

Too honest.

Her eyes widen, the smallest flicker—surprise... or something sharper.

I shift my stance, leaning an elbow on the railing like that single crack in my armor wasn't visible from orbit.

"If anyone suspects what you are," I say, voice low, measured,

"the Empire doesn't detain you, Alysa. They erase you."

She looks over the balcony, to the neon smear below.

"And you?" she asks quietly.

"You'd let them erase me?"

My answer is instinct:

"No."

Hard.

Immediate.

Undeniable.

Her breath catches—quiet, unguarded—and the sound hits me harder than it should.

Her head snaps toward me.

I don't look away—

but everything else inside me locks down.

Walls. Gates. Safeties.

"That doesn't mean you're safe," I add, tone shifting back to something cold and controlled.

"It only means I prefer to choose the variables in my vicinity."

A lie stretched thin over something too sharp to name.

"Tiberius..." she murmurs.

Not questioning.

Not accusing.

Just saying my name like a truth she wasn't meant to speak out loud.

I turn fully toward her.

Her pulse.

Her breath.

Her eyes.

Too close.

Too clear.

"You're not as unreadable as you think," she says softly.

I step away.

I have to.

Her gaze follows me—

sharp, perceptive, unwelcome in the places it reaches.

I walk toward the interior corridor.

Let her think what she wants.

Let her believe she can see me.

Let her believe she's wrong.

But the echo of our touch still burns across my skin, the echo of that unnamed thought—

and the truth I tried to swallow follows me down the hall:

Yes.

No.

Mine.

The only truths I've let slip in years.

And somehow—

she's the one who caught them.

Chapter 41: Rules of Pretending

Aly

The city feels wound tight tonight — every neon pulse like a heartbeat too close to the skin, every shadow listening. Even before the first word is spoken, the atmosphere presses close, watching.

Rain hasn't started yet, but the air in the transport hub lobby already feels charged—

like the city is holding its breath.

The lobby is all polished chrome, mirrored pillars, and soft blue path-lights embedded into the floor. Everything here gleams money. Efficiency. Surveillance. But the only thing that matters is the line Tiberius and I are walking: *public, visible, and believable.*

He walks a half-step ahead, posture crisp, the perfect Dominion officer escorting his new subordinate. Not touching me. Not looking at me. But the awareness between us is a thread—thin, taut, unignorable.

Eyes track us the moment we enter.

Executors. Their silver trim catches every stray light in the room, sending sharp reflections across the marble. Three of them flank the service desk like sharks dressed as bureaucrats.

One lifts his chin.

"Well, well. Commander Braxton," he says. "Didn't expect to see you in the transport hub this late at night... with company."

I keep my expression neutral. Not too stiff. Not too curious. Auditors are supposed to exist comfortably in the mid-ground between invisible and intimidating.

Tiberius gives the Executor a small nod—just respectful enough to avoid suspicion, just cold enough to remind everyone who he is.

"Training acquisition," he says. His voice is smooth glass, unbothered. "New internal auditor assigned to my division."

The Executor's gaze drags to me, slow and assessing.

"Verification?"

Tiberius doesn't blink. "Conduct your test."

The Executor smiles the way people do when they hope something goes wrong.

He turns to me.

"State the primary performance indicators for tier-three transport efficiency. And their expected variance."

Tiberius doesn't look at me.

He trusts me to lie for us.

Or he needs me to.

Either way, my pulse finds a steady rhythm.

I clasp my hands behind my back, like I've done this a thousand times.

"Transport efficiency is evaluated by four primary indicators," I say plainly. "Queue processing time, pod turnaround speed, transit accuracy, and personnel shift adherence. Variance should not exceed point-seven percent."

The Executor raises an eyebrow.

"Point-seven? The revised benchmarks are stricter."

He's baiting me.

He wants a crack in the story.

"Correct," I say. "But the revised benchmarks haven't been adopted by Commander Braxton's division yet. They're in pilot testing only. Request for implementation is pending final approval." I offer a small, bored shrug. "Still waiting on the Continuum's resource projections, last I checked."

The Executor blinks.

He wasn't expecting pushback with details.

Tiberius finally looks at me.

Not long. Not soft.

Just enough to be seen by the room.

"Accurate," he says.

His tone is razor-flat praise—Dominion-style approval.

It lands like a strike.

Something in the Executors shifts—subtle, stiffening. Recognition that I am not just his new hire.

I am *his*.

Or so it needs to look.

"Well," the lead Executor says slowly, "seems you've done your homework."

Tiberius tilts his head. "I don't keep deadweight."

The words should sting.

They don't.

Not when I can feel the subtext beneath them, that nearly invisible thread between us drawing tighter.

He gives me the smallest eyebrow raise that I catch out of the corner of my eye. I can tell I've impressed him, enough he breaks his performance.

The Executors step aside. "Proceed."

Tiberius moves first, expecting me to follow.

I fall into step, the two of us walking in perfect synchrony—mirrored strides, matched pace, a seamless lie with no seams visible.

For a moment, it feels frighteningly natural.

But I remind myself what this is.

A cover.

A performance.

A game with teeth.

Still, as we pass through the tall glass doors toward the private corridors, I hear the soft hiss of the first raindrops hitting the roof above us, delicate and precise.

Like the city is marking the moment.

The moment we stop walking separately.

The moment we become a single, believable lie.

The moment everything starts to feel... dangerous.

✦ ☽⋆☾ ✦

Tiberius

The sky opens above us like a confession the city didn't mean to spill. Rain softens every edge, blurs every line—and somehow sharpens the truth between us.

The rain has started again, a soft hiss against metal. The glow from the streets below turns the puddles the color of mercury. I lead Alysa through a maintenance access and up a narrow stairwell; the hatch clangs shut behind us.

The hum of the city fades—muted by height, rain, and the walls around this forgotten rooftop. Up here, it's just neon breathing through the mist and the raw, unfiltered quiet of two people who don't know if they're allies or threats.

I cross to the railing and lean my hands against it. My coat drips steadily. My heartbeat slows.

"This is where I come when the noise gets too loud."

I don't look at her. Haven't decided if I *can*.

"From up here, the empire looks almost honest. Like it's just light and weather, not everything underneath."

For a moment I listen—rain on steel, distant sirens, the pulse of neon in the puddles at my feet. When I turn, the city's glow catches in her eyes.

"You asked me once what makes me different. I'm not sure it does. But I don't like killing ghosts that still have something to say."

I gesture at the skyline—at the fake serenity of a machine pretending to be a city.

"So talk, Alysa. Off record. No rebellion. No empire. Just two people standing in the rain. What do you want to remember when all of this ends?"

And this time it isn't a test.

It's the most honest invitation I've ever offered anyone.

She exhales—shaking like she hadn't realized she was holding the breath hostage. She looks up at the sky and lets the rain hit her face like she's washing off whatever armor she hasn't admitted she's wearing.

✦ ☽⋆☾ ✦

Aly

Time feels warped here—suspended—as though the world below can't reach us long enough to interfere.

"I'm not sure I want to remember anything. But if I don't remember how will I learn to be better and show others the same? I want to remember that there is still good in this world, and I don't see it at all. Only in what I show, and hardly anyone sees it and least of all except it from me."

Rain runs down my face. Cold, clean. Honest. I brush my hair back and look at him—really look. He's watching me like he's seeing someone he didn't plan for.

"What about you?"

✦ ☽⋆☾ ✦

Tiberius

The rain eats silence in slow, steady bites, but somehow the quiet between us grows louder.

Her question hits harder than it should.

"That's the hardest part," I say quietly. "Remembering and still choosing to stay human."

My fingers curl against the rail.

"The empire teaches you to forget. It tells you that forgetting is cleaner, that it makes you efficient. But that's just another cage."

I breathe out, a half-smile that feels more tired than anything.

"What do I want to remember? That I had a choice once. That I wasn't just my father's orders wearing a nicer suit. That someone looked at me and saw a man, not a weapon."

The silence between us fills with rain, with things I'm not used to saying aloud.

"You shouldn't have shown me that there's still good out here. It's inconvenient. Makes it harder to keep pretending."

I look away, then back at her.

"You talk about showing people there's good left. Maybe that's what freedom looks like—remembering until it hurts and doing better anyway."

Another pause. Another quiet truth.

"For what it's worth... you're better at it than you think, Alysa."

✦ ☽⋆☾ ✦

Aly

Something shifts under my ribs—small, sharp, and terrifyingly human.

My arms wrap around myself almost unconsciously. I look down, suddenly sheepish.

"I have come to realize that no one sees the good the way I see it."

I force myself to meet his eyes.

"And for whatever it's worth, I've always seen a man, and not the weapon."

He goes still—*really* still. Not the trained stillness of control, but the startled, unguarded kind. The rain reflects against the metal at our feet, trembling with every drop.

✦ ☽⋆☾ ✦

Tiberius

Moments like this are dangerous—the kind that change things, whether either of us wants them to or not.

"You shouldn't say things like that to me," I manage, voice rougher than I intend. "It'll sound like forgiveness, and I don't know what to do with that."

A breath escapes me—an actual laugh, quiet and unpolished.

"Maybe that's what makes you dangerous, Alysa Carmichael. You walk through the same ruins as everyone else and still manage to see people instead of ruins."

I push a hand through my hair, water running down my wrist.

"You see good where there shouldn't be any. You saw it in me. I don't know if that makes you reckless or right, but it makes me want to try harder to deserve it."

The confession lands between us like a fragile truce.

"Let's start there. Not forgiveness. Just trying to be worth seeing."

"Maybe forgiveness is where we start," she says softly, stepping closer—not touching, but close enough to see every raindrop tracking down my face. "I have. And maybe that's why I haven't killed you when I could have a thousand times before."

She lets out a short breath of humor.

"I am most certainly reckless. And you deserve forgiveness."

My shoulders loosen, a small breath of relief slipping out like I didn't mean it to.

"That's reckless," I say, though there's no protest in it. "Forgiving someone who hasn't earned it yet."

"Never said I wasn't," she says.

I tilt my head, studying her through the rain.

"Maybe you're right. Maybe forgiveness isn't a prize, it's a beginning."

The skyline glows across my vision—glass towers like electric veins.

"If I'm different after this, it won't be because you spared me. It'll be because you made me remember what being spared feels like."

Quieter, more private:

"Maybe that's freedom, too."

When I meet her gaze again, there's a faint, genuine smile pulling at my mouth.

"Reckless suits you, Alysa. Don't lose that. It's the first thing that's ever made me think this city might still have a future."

I reach out—close but not touching—just enough to let the possibility hang between us like breath in cold air.

"Shall we call it a truce? For tonight at least?"

"A truce then," she says—and she take my hand.

Her hand in mine is warm despite the rain. Careful. Human. I close my fingers around hers slowly, afraid she'll slip away if I move wrong.

"A truce," I echo.

We stand there in silence for a heartbeat that feels longer than it should.

"Tomorrow, they'll all still want our heads. The Empire won't stop, and your rebels won't trust this. But right now..."

I glance at our joined hands, then back at her.

"...right now, the world isn't ending. That's enough."

I release her hand—slowly, reluctantly—then nod toward the stairwell.

The edge of a grin tugs at my mouth.

She grins back. Small and genuine and something in me breaks at the sight of it.

She steps ahead of me down the stairs, pausing at the landing.

"What do I call you then?"

For a moment, I consider dodging. But not tonight.

"Tiberius is what the empire built," I say. "The title they give when they want obedience."

I meet her at the bottom of the stairwell, walking beside her.

"Ty was the name my mother used before they scrubbed her from the records. That one's still mine."

Neon flickers through the mist as we step onto the alley.

"So if you want the truth, call me Ty. If you need the empire to listen, call me Tiberius."

"Alright, Ty," she says softly, and it cracks something in me the way she says my name. then she adds. "You can call me Aly, by the way."

✦ ☽⋆☾ ✦

Aly

The air between us feels changed—heavier, thinner, charged in a way that settles low in my ribs. The rain hasn't stopped, but it suddenly feels quieter, like the city itself is listening.

"Aly," he says.

My name isn't a whisper.

But it's quiet in the way a secret is quiet.

In the way something valuable tries not to shake.

Hearing it from him is an impact.

A hit.

A tether.

And suddenly we are standing too close with too much unsaid and too much already changed.

"...Aly," he says one final time, like he has to test it, to taste it, to accept that he's allowed to have one thing tonight that isn't built by Dominion.

There's heat under it.

And restraint.

And confusion.

And something dangerously close to hope.

I shift my weight, pulse kicking hard, and for just a heartbeat neither of us moves.

Not away.

Not toward.

Balanced on a knife's edge between what we are and what we're trying—and failing—to pretend we're not.

The rooftop seems to hold its breath with us.

The rain softens for half a second, like even the weather wants to see how this breaks.

Then the moment breaks, thin as glass.

Ty steps back half an inch. I feel the loss more than I want to.

He straightens his coat, smoothing water from the fabric, rebuilding the mask piece by piece even as it keeps slipping.

And I turn toward the roof hatch and towards lower streets, knowing he's a step behind me.

By the time we reach street level again, the city feels sharper. The rain falls harder, the air colder, the neon louder—as if everything knows something shifted on that rooftop.

I stop at the mouth of the alley, staring in the direction of my hideout. My chest tightens.

"I've been gone too long. If I don't get back, we'll have a riot soon."

It's meant to be light, but it comes out thinner, more fragile. Because I honestly don't know what I'm returning to.

Ty studies me with a tension he tries to hide behind stillness.

"You shouldn't walk alone," he says.

"And you shouldn't be seen with me."

His jaw ticks.

He hates that I'm right. And I hate that I notice it.

A heavy pause. A dangerous one.

"Don't get killed on your way home," he says, voice too flat to be casual.

"You either."

His eyes heat at that—an involuntary flicker, quickly suppressed.

"This truce won't mean anything if you throw yourself into the next fire you see."

"And it won't mean anything if you leave and pretend none of this happened."

That lands. Hard.

His breath stutters—barely—but enough to tell me he felt that.

"Aly—"

Warning.

Wanting.

Worried.

I step back first, though it hurts something I don't want to name.

"If you're going to change sides, you'll have to survive long enough to do it."

His mouth twitches—not a smile.

"And if you're going to forgive me, you'll have to come back alive so I can earn it."

Something catches in my throat.

I want to say *I already did... a long time ago* but I don't they stay lodged in my throat and I swallow them.

"Go," he says, low. "Before I do something reckless enough to ruin this entire agreement."

"You already did," I whisper. "You told me the truth."

We stand there in the rain, not moving, not speaking, both of us tethered to a moment we can't keep.

Then we turn.

He walks toward the Empire's upper sectors.

I walk toward the rebellion below.

And the truce burns warm in my hand long after he's out of sight.

I don't know when I will see him again, but when I do...

I trust that he won't kill me.

Because I can't kill him.

Chapter 42: Echoes in the Continuum

Ty

The lift drops me into the central spine of the Continuum like a stone hitting deep water.

Dark glass.

White light.

Silence engineered to suppress thought.

Aly is miles behind me by the time I reach the Continuum—

but somehow her footsteps feel closer than they should,

echoes I'm not supposed to hear, emotions I'm not supposed to have.

I force them down.

Not away.

Just far enough that I can breathe without giving anything away.

I tuck the memory of her hand into the deepest place I have—

not to keep it,

but to keep it from showing.

Dominion carved obedience into my bones,

but something shifted tonight.

A hairline crack.

A breath I wasn't meant to have.

Something in me keeps reaching for the moment on that rooftop—

not the words,

not the truce,

but the feeling.

And that...

isn't something obedience ever allowed.

The doors whisper open, and I step into my father's domain.

Dominion's data tower isn't a room.

It's a machine wearing a cathedral's bones—holographic streams cascading down the walls, panels humming with heartbeat-red diagnostics, the Continuum's core like a hanging star suspended from obsidian beams.

I stand at attention.

Mask on.

Breath tight.

Dominion doesn't turn when I enter.

He never needs to.

"Commander Braxton," he says, voice carrying through the chamber with that too-smooth resonance the Continuum gives him. "Your audit logs have been processed."

A strand of cold slides down my spine.

There it is.

The anomaly.

He gestures, and a holographic window flickers to life—Aly's erased record.

The one that should have been overwritten.

The one I made sure to bury.

I shouldn't feel anything about this.

But the sight of that flicker—

that surviving piece of her—

hits someplace I don't have a name for.

Not fear.

Not duty.

Something else.

It glows.

A ghost line.

A partial ID stamp.

A timestamp that shouldn't exist.

My chest tightens.

Not from fear of discovery—

I've lived inside fear so long it feels like gravity—

but from the realization that she shouldn't exist here at all.

And yet she does.

A ghost the Continuum couldn't erase,

the same way she never left the back of my mind.

I used to think I imagined her.

Now I'm not so sure.

Dominion tilts his head, studying the fractured data like a painting.

"You were in the vault tonight."

A statement, not a question.

"Yes, sir."

"And you brought a trainee."

My muscles lock. "Yes."

"Explain why her biometric signature appears only in the Continuum's residual cache, but not in any primary file."

There it is: the blade of the question.

Cold. Precise.

A test disguised as curiosity.

I breathe once.

Slow.

Measured.

The old version of me would have answered instantly—

clean, sharp, obedient.

But something tonight made hesitation seep into my circuitry.

I hate that he can probably hear it in the silence.

"Faulty subroutine," I say. "I triggered a latency bypass during the training demo. It corrupted the secondary logs."

A lie.

Clean.

Sharp.

Perfect.

My father taught me to lie only when ordered to.

But this lie came from me—

unbidden,

instinctive,

protective in a way that feels wrong and right in the same breath.

I don't do instinct.

Dominion carved it out of me years ago.

So whatever moved my tongue just now...

wasn't training.

It was something alive.

I don't recognize myself in this moment.

And that scares me more than my father ever has.

Dominion finally turns toward me.

Eyes like polished steel.

Expression unreadable.

"You bypassed protocol," he says.

"I optimized it."

"You corrupted the Continuum."

"I corrected for inefficiency."

A pause—thin, slicing.

His gaze presses into me, heavy as gravity.

"You take responsibility for the anomaly?"

"Yes, sir."

"Even if the anomaly is not yours?"

My pulse stutters in my throat.

Barely.

But enough.

He hears the crack.

He always hears them.

I brace for the instinct to obey—

the one that's ruled me since childhood—

but it doesn't rise fast enough.

Something else moves first:

the urge to shield her name from even existing in this room.

"I take responsibility," I repeat.

Another long silence.

Then Dominion nods once—slow, as though calculating.

"Very well."

He dismisses the hologram.

The ghost line vanishes in a flicker of blue light.

"Do not fail again," he says.

The words scrape along something raw inside me because I almost already did.

"No, sir."

"Go."

I turn sharply, the way he expects, the way I've been shaped to move—controlled, obedient, predictable.

But inside?

Inside my heart is still racing from the lie.

From the defiance.

From the knowledge that for the first time in my life, I chose to protect someone who isn't Dominion.

Someone who isn't me.

Someone who looked at me on a rooftop in the rain
and didn't see a weapon.

As the lift doors close around me, I realize something horrifying:

I didn't lie because I'm disloyal.

I lied because I finally *care* about something more than obedience.

Something more than survival.

Someone.

And that is the beginning of treason.

And yet, beneath all of it—
the conditioning,
the protocols,
the armor—
I feel something I'm not ready to name.

A presence like a warm handprint pressed on the inside of my ribs.

Aly.

The girl I tried to forget.

The one I never could.

Somewhere in the shadows of the tower walls, a hidden node hums to life—
a backchannel audit request initiating itself without my touch.

A shadow audit.

On me.

Chapter 43: The Spark and the Silence

Aly

The rain hasn't stopped since I left him.

It follows me down every level of the city, dripping through corroded grates and exposed cables, turning the old freight tunnels into rivers of light and shadow. The Undergrid breathes around me—generators coughing, overheated pipes hissing, rebels murmuring like the walls themselves have ears.

I should tell them where I've been.

What I saw.

What I did.

What I failed to do.

But every step I take toward the base feels heavier, like the night is clinging to my skin—not the rain, but **him**.

The way he said my name.

The way his mask cracked.

The way he stood too close and didn't raise a weapon.

My chest tightens.

I wasn't supposed to see any of that.

I wasn't supposed to feel *any* of that.

I slip into the old comm room—the one with the broken door and the half-dead console—because it's the only place down here that doesn't ask anything of me. It smells like dust and old circuitry. The lights buzz weakly overhead, flickering in a rhythm that feels too much like a heartbeat.

My heartbeat.

There's a recording node on the desk.

I don't think.

I just sit.

And press it on.

Static fuzzes through the speaker. When I speak, my voice comes out thin, cracked around the edges.

"Mercy is still mine."

It feels like a confession.

I rub my palms together, trying to stop the shaking that isn't from cold.

I don't say his name.

Not Ty.

Not Tiberius.

Not the name that tasted too soft on my tongue when he gave it to me.

I don't say *mother* either.

I don't say that I failed her tonight.

That I went into the vault alone to erase the last piece of her that Dominion still owns...

and I couldn't do it.

And he—the empire's heir—promised to do it instead.

A truce with the tyrant's son.

A vow from the one person I should never trust.

A vow I *do* trust anyway.

I lean back in the chair, staring up at the flickering lights, letting the truth settle like a bruise I can't hide.

"My whole life I've been told mercy gets people killed," I whisper. "But tonight... I didn't feel weak."

I close my eyes because the alternative is seeing his face again—rain streaking down his jaw, restraint trembling in his voice, the look he gave me when he said *Aly*, like the word itself was dangerous.

"If he can remember he's more than a weapon," I breathe, "then maybe I can remember I'm more than a ghost."

The console hisses softly.

I stop the recording before I spill anything that could ruin both of us.

No one here can know where I went tonight.

Or that I wasn't alone.

Or who I was with.

I stand, rolling my shoulders back until the weight settles where it belongs. Outside the room, the Undergrid groans—shifting metal, footsteps of rebels who'd tear the city apart if they knew I let Dominion's son stand beside me in the dark.

Maybe they should.

Maybe I should.

But I don't.

Not tonight.

Whatever tomorrow brings—riots, suspicion, war—at least for a moment on that rooftop, I felt something alive, something true, something I haven't allowed myself to feel in years.

Hope.

When I leave the room, the lights flicker.

I don't notice it.

The door seals behind me with a soft hydraulic hiss, and my footsteps fade into the corridor. The hum of the Undergrid swallows me whole.

But behind the closed door—

in the room I just walked away from—

a secondary screen I didn't touch blinks awake.

Harsh white text carves itself across the dark:

UNMARKED TRANSMISSION

SOURCE: UNKNOWN

SUBJECT: TOBIAS—ANOMALY FLAGGED

The message loops once.

Twice.

No one is there to see it.

No one is there to feel the cold spike running through the hidden lines of code.

I keep walking, rain thundering through the vents above me, unaware of the warning pulsing in the dark.

Had I stayed even one second longer, I would have seen the screen shudder—

the message vanish—

the room fall silent again, as if nothing had happened at all.

But I'm already gone.

And I have no idea whose secret is being hunted tonight.

His.

Or mine.

✦ ☽⋆☾ ✦

Ty

The city looks different in the rain.

Colder.

Sharper.

Honest in a way it never allows itself to be when the lights are dry.

I stand on the balcony outside my quarters in the Upper Citadel, coat soaked through, hands braced against the railing like it's the only thing keeping me upright. Water beads along the metal and falls in thin silver lines to the streets far below.

The Ion Veil pulses between the towers—electric veins running gold, blue, white—the city's heartbeat stitched into the night.

A cage disguised as a skyline.

The Continuum is quiet behind me.

Too quiet.

A predator's silence.

My father is somewhere in its corridors, watching, calculating, deciding what part of me to carve off next. I can still feel the weight of his scrutiny, like his gaze is a fingerprint pressed into the back of my skull.

But out here—in the rain, in the dark, where the world feels raw instead of curated—I can finally breathe.

Aly wouldn't survive up here.

The sector alone would kill her.

The air.

The surveillance.

The eyes trained to see ghosts and crush them.

And yet—

I close my eyes.

The world narrows.

The memory of her hand in mine is too warm.

Too grounding.

Too real.

The memory of her voice—quiet but unbroken—echoes like a frequency I wasn't built to hear.

And beneath all of it, something older stirs.

Recognition.

Like a puzzle piece shifting into a place I didn't know was empty.

I whisper her name, soft enough that the rain almost steals it.

"Aly."

It isn't a vow.

Not exactly.

But it feels like one.

Because saying it is the first thing I've done tonight that belongs entirely to me.

Not loyalty.

Not rebellion.

Just truth.

A truth the Empire didn't program.

A truth Dominion can't erase.

A truth I didn't know I was capable of feeling.

Somewhere miles below, she's walking back into danger she refuses to name.

Somewhere behind me, a shadow audit is already digging into my digital pulse, tearing apart the lies I wrapped around her existence.

I should regret everything.

I should sever this—whatever this is—before it becomes real enough to get us both killed.

But when I open my eyes, the Ion Veil reflects back at me:

cold light, hot pulse, fractured sense of self—

and all I can think of is the way she looked at me.

Like she saw the man.

Not the weapon.

No one has ever looked at me like that.

Not once.

Not ever.

My hands curl against the railing.

Not from anger.

From the impossible urge to hold on to something I don't deserve.

For the first time in my life, silence feels heavy.

Charged.

Like a storm waiting for the right moment to break.

Above me, the city hums with machinery and politics sharp enough to cut bone.

Below me, the Undergrid grinds with ghosts who refuse to be erased.

And somewhere between those two worlds, one fragile truth holds steady in the rain:

I am not alone in this anymore.
Two ghosts under the same storm,
each guarding the other's truth,
each standing on opposite ends of a city built to keep them apart,
each whispering a name the world was never meant to hear.
And somewhere deep in the Continuum's core,
a silent alert flickers:
ANOMALY CONFIRMED.
TRACKING INITIATED.
The spark has already lit the fuse.
The silence will not hold.

Epilogue

Dominion

The Continuum's inner chamber hums like a sleeping beast.

Dominion stands alone before the suspended lattice of data-veins, hands clasped behind his back, eyes half-lidded in the soft blue glow. He does not need full attention for this. The system thinks for him. Breathes for him. Obeys him.

A single pulse of red cuts through the blue.

Anomaly detected.

Dominion's head tilts a fraction—the closest he comes to showing curiosity.

The data thread stretches, branches, resolves into a profile.

SUBJECT: COMMANDER TIBERIUS BRAXTON

DEVIATION: UNAUTHORIZED LOG CORRECTION

BEHAVIORAL IRREGULARITY: ELEVATED

The Continuum waits for his command.

Dominion does not speak immediately.

He studies the fractured log the way a surgeon studies an incision—not surprised to see blood, only evaluating whether it came from the right vein.

His expression never shifts.

"Isolate the catalyst," he says.

The system obeys without hesitation.

A second thread unwinds, glitching, incomplete—someone the Continuum tried to erase, and failed.

UNMATCHED BIOMETRIC TRACE

ORIGIN: UNKNOWN

SIGNAL: PERSISTENT

A ghost.

Dominion watches the pattern flicker, and for the first time tonight, lifts his chin.

"Interesting," he murmurs.

Not angry.

Not threatened.

Interested.

He extends a hand; the hologram lowers into his palm like a captured heartbeat.

"Track both anomalies," he orders. "But do not intervene yet."

The Continuum acknowledges the command.

"Observation first," Dominion continues. "Interference only when the fault line becomes useful."

He closes his fist, folding the light into darkness.

"And it will."

The lights fade back to blue.

The red pulse vanishes.

Dominion stands perfectly still, a silhouette carved against the vast machinery of the Empire—a man watching the beginnings of fracture, amused by the inevitability of it.

He turns the ghost fragment of data between his fingers, the light flickering like a heartbeat that refuses to die.

"Lara..."

Her name leaves him in a breath that is almost a memory—almost.

Then the softness curdles.

"You should have stood beside me."

A low, bitter hum undercuts the words.

"You were meant to."

He studies the flickering shard as if it were her face—

the defiance,

the refusal,

the choice that robbed him of something he still believes *should have been his.*

"But instead, you ran."

His voice drops, silk wrapped around a blade.

"You built a rebellion you were never strong enough to lead.

And you died for it."

The shard dims.

He closes his fist around it, the light smothering between his fingers.

"Now your mistake burns on without you," he murmurs.

"And I will let it burn itself away... just like you did."

He turns from the consoles, satisfied.
Certain.
Blind.
Because the one thing Lara left behind—
the one person he never knew existed—
is still out there.
And tonight, she walked beside his shadow.

Acknowledgments

To my children—you have been my light and my anchor. You remind me every day what it means to keep going, to dream boldly, and to stay grounded in love.

To my mom—thank you for encouraging me, even in the moments when I doubted myself. Your belief carried me further than you know.

To my sister—who patiently listened to my endless ramblings and half-formed ideas, even when the threads of this story made no sense outside my head. Your quiet support mattered more than words.

To my beta readers—both of you are phenomenal. Your insight, honesty, and care for these characters made this story stronger than it ever could have been alone. And because you are both older than I am, I trusted you instinctively to see the layers beneath the surface—to catch what mattered, and to tell me the truth when it counted. Thank you for reading this story first and holding it with such care.

This book is as much yours as it is mine.

Author's Note

You made it to the end.

You survived the Empire. For now. Good.

You watched two dangerous people take their first step toward defying the world that built them.

Thank you.

Ghosts of the Empyrium poured out of me like a fuse catching flame. I wrote this book with my whole chest, every scar, every spark, every unhinged idea that whispered "*write me.*" Aly and Ty burned through the page faster than I could type and refused to let go.

If they carved their way into you too, then welcome.

You're one of us now.

Call to Action:

If you want to see this series rise, you can help by:

dropping a review (it matters more than you think)

sharing your favorite lines or edits

joining my newsletter for early peeks at book two

Your voice builds this rebellion.

Your reviews keep the fire burning.

See you in *Shadows of the Empyium*, where the truce... doesn't stay quiet for long.

—Alysabeth Vale

About the Author

Alysabeth Vale writes like she's on fire and refuses to apologize for it.

A storyteller since she was fourteen, she builds entire worlds in days, writes at a velocity that should not be possible, and pours every scar, spark, and heartbeat into the characters she creates.

She doesn't write because it's easy.

She writes because it's the one place she feels most alive.

Driven by instinct, emotion, and a mind wired for story, she forges narratives that hit hard, linger long, and refuse to be forgotten. Every book she writes is crafted with the same intensity she demands from her characters—raw, honest, and utterly fearless.

Now she's building a publishing empire from the ground up, one book, one reader, one feral character arc at a time.

If her books hit you in the chest... good.

That means they're doing their job.

Sneak Peek at The Empyrium Chronicles Book 2: Shadows of the Empyrium.

Walking Into The Wolf's Den

Ty

Dominion's summons hits my terminal before sunrise.

No preamble.

No seal.

Just a line that might as well be a blade:

Report. Bring the analyst.

The words burn in pale blue across the screen.

I stare at them for exactly three seconds.

Any longer is hesitation.

Any less is obedience.

My reflection ghosts over the text in the dark glass—eyes flat, jaw tight, hair still damp from the shower. I look like him in this light.

I hate that.

In the quiet hallway outside, I hear soft movement. Aly, waking. The faint pad of bare feet. The whisper of fabric.

Of all the mornings for him to decide he wants a demonstration...

I lock the terminal, step out of my room, and cross the short distance to hers.

The door is cracked open. She's already dressed—analyst black, hair braided high and tight, hands braced on the edge of the dresser like she's steadying herself against a fall no one else can see.

She looks up as I enter.

She reads my face before I speak.

Her spine tightens.

"What happened?"

I don't waste time.

"Dominion summoned," I say. "He wants a report."

She exhales once—sharp, contained. "Of course he does."

I nod once, the hard part still coming.

"And he wants you there."

Aly stiffens the second she hears it.

"I can hide," she insists. "Blend in with your officers. I'll keep my hood up—"

"No."

It comes out too sharp.

I rein it back, but the word hangs there between us like a command I didn't mean to weaponize.

Her eyes narrow.

I force my voice down, smoothing the edges.

"You don't hide from Dominion," I say. "He'll notice. He *always* notices."

She crosses her arms, weight dropping into one hip in a way that says she's already assessing angles, exits, weapons.

"I'm not letting him pick me apart. I can handle myself."

"I know you can."

And god, I do.

I've watched her move through chaos like it obeys her.

I've seen her gamble with her life in the Vault and win.

I've watched her stand in front of me on a rooftop and choose to trust me anyway.

That's the problem.

If she goes in raw, if she snaps, if she lets the ash commander bleed through the analyst mask even once—Dominion will see it. He always does.

"I know you can," I repeat, quieter. "That's not the point."

Her jaw flexes.

"What *is* the point then, Ghost?" she asks. "That I stand there and let him drag me under a microscope while you smile and nod?"

"That you walk out," I say. "Alive."

We hold a deadlocked stare long enough to start a war.

Her eyes search my face like there's a confession I haven't said yet. There is. I don't let it out.

Finally, I exhale.

"...Fine. But stay behind me. And don't speak unless spoken to."

Aly smirks.

The expression is all teeth and defiance and history I don't know yet.

"Oh, that'll go well."

She's right.

It won't.

But I don't have time to argue with her stubbornness when I'm trying to keep us both in one piece.

"Get your boots," I say. "And leave anything overtly Undergrid in the room. Dominion doesn't miss fabric patterns."

She rolls her eyes, but she moves—slinging her coat on, adjusting the collar, checking hidden blades I pretend not to see.

"I thought you said he always notices," she mutters.

"He does," I say. "But I've learned to give him a curated list."

She snorts under her breath at that, but there's tension in her shoulders she can't hide.

We walk down the hallway together.

Side by side.

Too close.

Not close enough.

In the lift, the mirrored walls reflect us back: Lord Braxton and his analyst. Empire and rebellion. Wolf's son and the girl he should have turned in weeks ago.

The doors slide shut.

The car hums to life.

Aly watches the floor numbers rise, then glances at me from under her lashes.

"Does he know?" she asks quietly.

"Know what?"

"That you lied for me," she says. "In the Vault. In your report. In Sector Twelve. Take your pick."

"He suspects," I say. "He always suspects. That's his default state."

She studies me for a long second.

"And you're not... worried?"

My mouth twitches into something that isn't quite a smile.

"Of course I'm worried," I say. "I'm not suicidal."

I pause.

"But I'm more worried about what he'll do if you're not there when he expects you to be."

She goes very still at that.

Not offended.

Not cowed.

Just... recalibrating.

"And if I say no?" she asks.

"If you say no," I answer, "I walk into that room alone. He dissects every log and every decision from this week, finds the weak point, and pulls until something breaks. Either the lie... or me."

A beat.

"And once he breaks me," I add, "he will start looking for what I was hiding."

Her throat works around a swallow.

The silence stretches, thick and heavy.

She doesn't owe me this.

I know that.

She owes me nothing.

But she's the only person who knows exactly how deep this lie goes.

And I have the sickening feeling that if I walk into Dominion's chamber alone, I'll come out as something even less human than I already am.

The lift dings.

Upper command levels.

No more time.

Aly inhales, sharp and steady.

Her chin lifts.

"Fine," she says. "I'll play the analyst."

Her eyes harden—steel over flame.

"But if he pushes too far, Ty... I'm not promising I won't bite back."

The worst part?

I want her to.

www.ingramcontent.com/pod-product-compliance
Lightning Source LLC
LaVergne TN
LVHW100520110826
845146LV00002B/709

* 9 7 9 8 9 9 4 5 2 8 4 1 9 *